Dating CHAOS

A Model MD Novella

D.W. Brooks

Cover design by 100covers.com

Publisher's Cataloging-in-Publication data

Names: Brooks, D. W., author.
Title: Dating chaos : a model MD novella / D. W. Brooks.
Description: Houston, TX: Life: The Reboot LLC, 2024.
Identifiers: LCCN: 2024913714 | ISBN: 979-8-9890807-5-5 (paperback) | 979-8-9890807-4-8 (ebook)
Subjects: LCSH Physicians--Fiction. | Dating--Fiction. | Family--Fiction. | African American women--Fiction. | Atlanta (Ga.)--Fiction. | Romance fiction. | Love stories. | BISAC FICTION / Romance / African American & Black | FICTION / Family Life / General | FICTION / Medical
Classification: LCC PS3602 .R66 D38 2024 | DDC 813.6--dc23

Printed in Houston, TX USA.

Dedication

To my husband, who taught me that dating didn't have to be hard or chaotic.

Author's Note

This story contains explicit content and topics that may be sensitive to some readers. For a more detailed topic list, please scan the QR code or visit https://authordwbrooks.com

Dating CHAOS

Prologue

<hr>

On New Year's Eve, the front doorbell buzzed, reverberating throughout the Buckhead homestead in Atlanta.

The noise startled Jamison Jones Scott and her mother, Margaret Jameson Scott, as they talked in Jamie's bedroom. "It's almost eight in the morning. Are you expecting someone this early?" Jamie asked.

Margaret found herself at a loss. "No. The desserts for the party are being delivered later. Are *you* expecting someone?"

Jamie leaned over to her nightstand and picked up her coffee that her mother had brought to her a few minutes before. "Of course not. I wouldn't invite anyone over before eight for any reason!"

Crossing to the bedroom door, Margaret heard voices downstairs—one, she recognized from the past. Baffled and perturbed, she faced Jamie, realizing her husband

Gregory had allowed the familiar voice inside their home. Quietly, she left Jamie's room to eavesdrop.

"What's wrong, Mother?" Jamie inquired as she sat her coffee cup on the nightstand to trail after her. Margaret stopped short at the top of the stairs when she saw the early-morning visitor, and Jamie ran into her back.

"Geez! What is *wrong*, Mother?" Jamie grumbled but quieted when she observed the dismay on her mother's face. She turned her attention to the bottom of the stairs.

Gregory was talking to a short, stout woman, whose back was to the pair. Being over six feet tall, Gregory easily spotted his wife and daughter over their guest's head as soon as they had left the bedroom.

"Oh, hi, dear. I'm glad you're here. I have to get to work, but you have a surprise guest," Gregory called up to his wife, with an odd emphasis on the word 'surprise'.

At that point, the visitor turned around. Margaret gasped and tightly gripped the banister when she realized their guest was her older sister, Eleanor Jameson Drake. Instantly, the resemblance between Margaret and her sibling was obvious to Jamie. However, Margaret's face expressed horror, while Eleanor appeared hopeful.

And honestly, in this situation, hope was a tall order.

Eleanor, Margaret, and their three other siblings grew up in Alabama during the '50s and '60s in a well-to-do home with their African American physician father, and their homemaker mother. Obviously, white supremacy, racism, and desegregation were significant issues at the time, but their parents worked to shield their children from as much of the brutality of life as possible. Eleanor was four years older than Margaret, but the two sisters had been extremely close when they were younger. Even as they got older, and their life paths diverged, they could still carry on conversations, even if they were often combative ones. At least, that was until their relationship completely broke down eighteen years ago.

That had been the last voluntary conversation between Eleanor and Margaret. Their last conversation took place twelve years ago when their father, Alexander, passed away (their mother, Elaine, had passed away two years before). And the conversations around the funeral plans were *forced*. It was obvious Margaret only spoke to the family—especially Eleanor—out of obligation. And as soon as that responsibility ended, she was gone—incommunicado.

Now Eleanor was here on Margaret's doorstep—unexpected and unwelcome. With a hope of righting some previous wrongs. Hope that was prompted by reading an internet article by chance one morning a few days prior as she searched for early New Year's sales online at her kitchen table.

She had come across an article about the status of a kidnapping/murder case in Atlanta. The headline of this seven-day-old article wasn't that interesting, but the name of the kidnap victim and the affiliated company made her stop doomscrolling: Jamison Jones Scott.

That was her niece—a niece she hadn't seen in person

in almost twenty years. Eleanor quickly scanned the first few paragraphs for further details. The authorities hadn't solved the case, and the article had no comments from anyone in the family. She quickly mentioned it to her husband of ten years, Harvey Drake.

Harvey snorted and shook his head, putting his newspaper down. "You haven't talked to your sister since your parents died, and not very often before then. So, she's in the news? *And*?"

Eleanor cocked her head to the side. "Someone kidnapped her daughter *two* weeks ago. This was a follow-up article, noting that the perpetrator was still at large."

"*So*?"

"I think she would need some support, right? Her child almost died. I need to talk to her."

"Why? If she didn't call you, maybe she didn't want you to know. Or she didn't *care* if you knew. I wouldn't bother her. It sounds like she has enough to deal with," Harvey replied. He slid his glasses down on his nose and started reading his paper again.

Harvey answered in a nonchalant manner because he had had this same conversation with Eleanor throughout their entire marriage. Eleanor often expressed her desire to reconcile with her sister, but then she never followed through. Harvey believed that was a wise choice.

The conversation between the two spouses died there, but unlike during the previous iterations of this talk, Eleanor felt particularly motivated. She had been a different person eighteen years ago. Her first marriage had been on the rocks. She spent most of her time drunk, while she partied, flirted—and more—with eligible and ineligible men alike. Eleanor had just taken what she wanted, no matter who got rolled over in the process. Either way, she wasn't a nice person back then.

Margaret had gotten caught under those wheels...

After her divorce, things had changed for Eleanor. The rich ass she had been married to had moved on to his newest trophy wife. Her only child rarely spoke to her, probably for the same reason that Margaret didn't speak to her either. With her change in circumstances, she now lived like a more respectable, middle-aged woman.

She and her sister weren't getting any younger. Eleanor needed to fix this rift.

But how? Margaret obviously wouldn't call her, even if she needed help. Perhaps Eleanor needed to just show up unannounced in Atlanta.

And so she did...

"Hi, Margaret. It's been a long time. I came to visit, since you didn't let us know your daughter was OK." Noticing Jamison standing behind her mother, Eleanor paused. It had been years since she had laid eyes on her niece—even longer than the last time she had seen her sister. Jamison had been a teenager then; she looked the same but different. So did Margaret.

"Jamison, what a horrible experience you went through. I'm eager to learn all the details, and how you're handling it," Eleanor said. Then she paused, waiting for Margaret's response to her greeting. Her southern accent was evident, stronger than Margaret's or Gregory's. "You look good as always, Margaret," Eleanor added, switching her attention back to her sister.

Dazed, Margaret descended the stairs and hugged her sister briefly. "You look well, too, Eleanor." Margaret paused a moment before she asked, finally finding her resolve, "So, can you tell me what *the hell* you are doing here?"

Chapter 1

The day before New Year's Eve, the sun peeked over the horizon as Jamison awoke to her alarm. She wasn't a fan of alarms, but without them, she'd sleep until noon. But, staying in bed didn't pose a problem right now. Since returning to Atlanta, she had neither a job nor any specific places to go.

Jamie swung her long legs over the edge of the bed and stopped to think. A lot had happened since she had returned home after four years abroad. When she departed, Jamie had left a vast amount of wreckage behind after breaking off her engagement, turning down a perfect job at a popular dermatology clinic, and walking out on a vicious argument with her mother. During those years away, she worked with medical relief organizations in Africa and tried to get herself together. On her return, Jamie had originally planned to rectify some of the damage she had caused when she left without a goodbye to her fiancé, friends, and family. She wanted to mend things, to talk to everyone, and explain her side...

But it hadn't gone as planned. Her brother Jon had informed their mother of Jamie's expected return date, and Margaret had then planned a gigantic birthday bash (for herself), which warped into a pseudo-welcome-home party. Their mother had also invited Jamie's ex-fiancé, her estranged best friend, and many others.

So uncomfortable...

On top of that, on her first night back, someone had killed an employee at her parents' forensic lab business in the company parking lot. Jamie, attempting to assist in the case, had found herself bound in the back of an RV with the killer and his associates. Fortunately, these kidnappers were the most incompetent group of captors around. They had no escape plan or any way to collect a ransom—and they didn't like or trust one another. She had survived the horror of those hours, escaping with only a few bruises, scrapes, and a healthy helping of PTSD.

Jamie had already restarted therapy.

The only positive outcomes from her return so far were the slight improvement in her relationships with her mother and sister Jillian, and her burgeoning relationship with a detective, Nick Marshall, who had helped solve the murder.

The thought of Nick energized her, propelling her out of bed. Her new therapist had suggested exercise as part of her therapy regimen, but it was difficult with how overbearing her family had become since the kidnapping. To follow her therapist's recommendations and to placate her parents, Jamie took walks each morning around the private, gated Buckhead community where her parents lived. It was a momentary escape from her mother's watchful eye.

Typically, during each walk, Jamie would run into one or more of her parents' neighbors. She enjoyed interacting with adults who weren't members of her family, even though sometimes those meetings led to gossip. Jamie knew some of that gossip pertained to her. And often, an acquaintance would relay a juicy tidbit and then abruptly stop talking or—more awkwardly—try to change the subject when they realized the rumors they were spreading were about *her*.

How embarrassing...

Despite these hiccups, Jamie had to admit her daily walks improved her mindset, even on the mornings after she had nightmares.

Jamie reached into her chest of drawers, locating a long-sleeved burgundy top and matching leggings. She quickly changed from her flannel pajamas to her workout gear, making a valiant search for her purple puffer jacket that her brother Jon bought her for Christmas. It was probably in the kitchen or the study, because she stayed downstairs as late as possible most evenings. Anything to avoid hours of tossing and turning on the nights she struggled to fall asleep. Her sleep habits were a mess right now.

Grabbing a stretchy beanie, she headed out of her bedroom, and held the stair banister for balance as she went downstairs. Party decorations still adorned the railings of the winding stairs, but with everything that happened, no one had cleaned anything up from her mother's birthday party. Since Margaret had planned a small gathering for tomorrow night, it surprised her that her mother hadn't taken care of refreshing the decorations already. Margaret liked order.

As soon as the young woman hit the bottom step, Margaret walked out of her bedroom suite.

She was waiting for me, Jamie thought. Instead of showing irritation, Jamie plastered a bright smile on her face. She had resigned herself to dealing with the excessive concern for a while. She couldn't fault her mother for that.

Besides, Jamie knew the fragile peace between her mother and herself would not last: Jamie and Nick had planned their first date for tonight.

During the case, she and the detective flirted and fought. They even made out at Margaret's party. *If her mother only knew*! Her siblings had discovered them in a state of almost-public indecency. Fortunately, it wasn't their mother who found them...that might have been an ugly scene.

After her kidnapping, Nick and Jamie agreed to have a proper date to determine if their intense attraction could turn into something more. There was no rush, so the date could wait until she had gotten some rest and had time to recover. They also had to work around holiday plans. Nick already had out-of-town plans for his holiday vacation, but he was returning to Atlanta today. They wanted to have a nice, quiet dinner tonight. Since it was the day before New Year's Eve, they hoped the restaurants wouldn't be too crowded.

Margaret would hate that idea for two reasons: she didn't want Jamie to leave the house, and she didn't want her to date Nick. There was some snobbery involved in that opinion, but Margaret wanted a say in Jamie's relationship decisions. She thought she knew better about what would make Jamie happy.

It was a problem.

"Good morning, Mother. How are you?" Jamie asked as she spotted her purple jacket hanging on the back of a kitchen chair.

"Good morning, Jamison. How did you sleep?" Margaret asked as she gave her daughter a gentle hug before she could get into the kitchen. As she wrapped her arms around her eldest, she noted Jamie had lost a few pounds since her ordeal. Jamie had a history of disordered eating, and Margaret was worried about a relapse.

Not much got past Margaret in her house, though—at least, that's what she claimed. Her children would beg to differ. Margaret was aware of Jamie's nightmares after the kidnapping but kept it to herself. Sometimes, Margaret heard noises from Jamison's room during late-night trips to the kitchen. Since she was an adult, both Gregory and Margaret wanted Jamison to have the freedom* to live her life as she saw fit (*within reason, according to Margaret). Jamison had explicitly told her mother that she preferred to address her problems alone. Her parents knew she had begun therapy; their daughter didn't want to worry them further.

Another thing that did not get past Margaret in her house: she sensed Jamie had a date planned with that detective one day soon. Margaret wondered how Jamison would handle telling her about that.

"I had a decent night, and before you ask, I don't see the therapist again until the New Year. Now, I'm going walking," Jamie replied as her mother followed her into the kitchen. "Are you going into the office today?" she continued, slipping on her jacket.

Uncomfortable silence. Jamie already knew her mother had a meeting at their forensics lab today; she simply wanted to deflect the conversation so she could escape without an argument.

"As you *already* know, I have a meeting, so I am going in for a few hours. What are you doing today?" the older woman asked. "Why don't you grab something to eat before you go out? You need to keep up your strength." Margaret pulled out some Kona coffee from a cabinet. "At least have a cup of coffee and a piece of fruit," she added, turning on the coffeemaker.

Jamie wanted to avoid a fight, and a cup of coffee would be nice. So, she entered the kitchen and sat on one of the bar stools at the L-shaped island. Margaret pulled down two mugs from an upper cabinet and retrieved the creamer from the refrigerator. She also handed Jamie a banana, which she accepted.

Taking a bite, Jamie avoided her mother's initial question and countered with one of her own. "Where's

Dad?"

"He has a breakfast meeting with some techs in the office. They need to discuss some more changes, since all that criminal behavior occurred," Margaret noted wryly as she got herself a cup of yogurt and brought the coffeepot over to pour each of them a cup. "The consultant has several suggestions that we need to wade through. Your father would like your help with that when life has settled down more."

After the murder, kidnapping, and other improprieties in the office, Gregory and Margaret had hired a consultant to make security changes and protocol updates. The death of Rachel Thorne, the employee, in the lab's parking lot did not occur solely because of anything happening at the office, but the lax security had aggravated the situation. It turned out that Rachel and another employee, Tatiana Daniels, who was part of the gang that kidnapped Jamie, had questionable issues in their past that neither Margaret nor Gregory had uncovered during the interview process. That lapse had almost cost them their daughter.

Jamie finished her banana and took a sip of her coffee. She liked this brand of coffee so much that she often would drink it black. She almost felt relaxed this morning, chatting with her mother. No discussion about sensitive topics. At least her mother did not ask her about her interest in working with them today.

She remained unsure about working for her parents, even part time. Upon her return stateside, her dad had offered Jamie an opportunity to consult and possibly take over the then-planned business expansion. She had been actively considering working with her father to learn more about the company. But now...

"Although you don't have to worry about that right now," her mother continued.

Spoke too soon. Unfortunately, Jamie could see the direction this was headed—to a lecture about being careful. The mood in the kitchen had been pleasant, and she wanted to get outside before it grew hostile.

"Excuse me, Mother. I *really* need to get going."

Surprisingly, her mother didn't battle her.

After Jamie left the house through the front door, Margaret remained in her chair, sipping her coffee. It had only been two weeks since the whole kidnapping mess. She had maintained a tight rein on her emotions, as she tried to keep a tighter rein on her very-grown daughter. Margaret couldn't help it. If the kidnappers had been even minimally competent, they would have killed Jamison, making her disappear forever.

Margaret was grateful that Jamison acknowledged the danger she had been in. She welcomed that concession. Their relationship was better than it had been in a long time.

Which probably wouldn't last.

Of course, Margaret found this disappointing. The relationship between Margaret and her eldest daughter had been nonexistent while Jamie was overseas. But even before then, since Jamison was sixteen, communications between the two had been strained. After Margaret found out that Jamison was pregnant by her older, drug-addicted, photographer boyfriend, Margaret had treated Jamison like the young woman couldn't make a single decision right. To her mother's relief, Jamie hadn't actively defied her and had tried to make her mother happy for years. Until she didn't. When Jamie ended her engagement, which Margaret thought was a silly choice, it led to a blowout argument that had contributed to Jamie's departure.

When Jamie had returned from her four-year-long trip, Margaret was happy to have her back, so she tried her best to not rock the boat. But she still had plans for her daughter. She believed that Jamison still had time to get married, have a few kids, and get her life back on track. Margaret took another sip of her coffee. Jamison probably didn't agree, but what did she know about her own life?

But since the kidnapping...

Margaret had never in her life been so terrified as she had been while her daughter was missing. But despite her fear, she acknowledged that her personality and behavior remained unchanged. She maintained her strong opinions and openly expressed whatever was on her mind. Sometimes Margaret considered easing up on Jamison a bit—except that Detective Marshall was sniffing around. And that would not do...

Chapter 2

I sabella Saldana gently closed the front door to a spacious brick home in Druid Hills, a suburb of Atlanta. Once outside, she took a couple of dance steps, humming the song "Love on Top" by Beyonce. Perfect sentiment for how she felt right now—a little drunk in love. And there was one guy to thank for this giddy feeling.

The young woman didn't have a key to the house, so the source of her newfound passion, Jonathan Scott, would have to lock the deadbolt from his home alarm app. Jonathan had an early meeting, and had left before her alarm went off, kissing her cheek while she slept. While it was sweet that he let her sleep, she wished that he had woken her up. She smiled to herself, thinking about Jon. She would have liked to send him off with a proper goodbye. Perhaps she could take the edge off that longing with a quick call?

While standing on the front porch, Isabella fished out

her cell phone. The Atlanta morning was a little chilly, so she pulled her white cashmere coat closer around her. The cool breeze whipped her straight, dark brown hair around her head with the ends stinging her face as the phone rang. She regretted not asking to borrow one of Jon's beanies before he left.

"Hello there, Isabella." Jon smoothly answered her call on the first ring. He liked the way her full name—not her nickname, Izzy—rolled off his tongue. It was sexy...like her. He liked how this relationship was unfolding, although it was still new.

"Hi, yourself!" she replied, happily doing a half-turn in place. "I wanted to tell you I just left the house. Lock your deadbolt."

"You didn't have to call me for that. You could have texted me," Jon replied, leaning back in his office chair. He was glad she had called, but he liked to needle her a bit.

"You don't like the sound of my voice?" she asked, saucily. "You don't have to hear it anymore. I will be as quiet as a mouse the next time we're in bed." Isabella knew he was just giving her a difficult time, but she liked to play along. Playing along with Jon could be fun, as she found out last night!

In a plaintive tone, Jon replied, "Oh, please don't do that. I like the way you *scream* my name." He smirked to himself. "Are we still on for tonight?"

"Of course," Isabella answered. "I'll call you later to let you know when I can leave the office." Stepping off the small porch, she added, "I might call you later just to say hi."

He laughed as they disconnected the call.

This relationship might work, he noted. *It was about time!*

As Isabella hurried to her car, another smile spread across her face. She was floating on air—caught in the early flushes of new love.

New love was a bitch...and a risk.

Originally from south Texas, Isabella worked for an accounting firm, and had done some consulting for Margaret and Gregory Scotts' forensic laboratory. That led to a fix-up with their son, Jonathan. Margaret had described him as thirty-three years old, six-foot-three, handsome, and an architect—one date seemed like a safe bet. His reputation as a player was widely known around town, yet women often believed they could tame the elusive bachelor. Their first date had been three weeks ago at Margaret's birthday/welcome home shindig for Jon's older sister Jamison, the model/physician.

The date had gone well, and so far, things were clicking between them.

Last night's date was magical, too, and everything was nearly perfect. As a prelude to his New Year's Eve surprises, Jon had made grand plans for last night. He'd taken Isabelle to a comedy show, then on a carriage ride downtown, and then to Polaris, the rotating bar at the downtown Hyatt Hotel. The scenery was beautiful, the setting was so romantic; they barely made it home before ripping each other's clothes off. The sex had been intense and amazing. Everything about the evening was unforgettable.

Right now, she just felt lucky. Despite her difficult background and the challenges she faced to become an accountant, Isabelle always had hopes of finding a fairytale relationship. Everything in her life seemed easy and calm. However, a small part of her remained wary. Something in the back of her mind kept reminding her that if something seemed too good to be true, it probably was. But she was going to ride the thrill for now—pun intended.

Isabella unlocked the car with her key fob, opened the door, and started to swing her purse into the passenger seat. Something caught her purse on the backswing, which threw Isabella off balance. Whirling around, Isabella found herself face-to-face with an attractive woman sporting a short burgundy bob.

Well, not actually face-to-face—the woman was around six inches taller than Isabella's five-foot frame. The other woman wore a brown leather jacket and a pair of leather jeans, but she looked young.

"What the hell? What are you doing?" Isabella asked as she ripped her purse back from the unknown woman. She had pepper spray in her purse, which she should have already had in her hand. *Damn*!

"Sorry. I shouldn't have snuck up on you like that. You were about to hit me with your bag as you swung it," the young woman replied.

"Sorry?" Isabella asked, sarcasm dripping from her voice. She clutched her bag to her chest and placed her hand inside, digging around for her pepper spray canister. "I have pepper spray! Back up!" She snapped and eyed the woman from head to toe. "Who are you, and what do you want?"

The woman took two steps backwards, holding her hands up in front of her. "OK. Sorry, again. My name is Rena. Jon and I date," she stated.

The world stopped on its axis.

Date. D*ate? WTF? Too good to be true*...a little voice danced around in Isabella's head.

"What?" Isabella asked as she tried to maintain her composure. She searched the young woman's face and found no evidence of guile. Her heart sank further.

Rena stumbled over her words during her reply. "I meant we used to date, but now we only have sex when he wants it."

Isabella felt as if she was looking through a tunnel. *How could she be so blind?*

Hold it together—get some details, she told herself. "When was this? When did you last sleep together? Jon and I have been together every night for the last two weeks."

"I meet him during the day most days, or whenever he wants me. We are meant to be together."

That explanation made little sense, as she had been to Jon's office during the day several times since the pair started dating, but Isabella also knew about Jon's history. After experiencing such ecstasy a few minutes before, suddenly, the ground was crumbling beneath her feet. *Why would this girl tell her this*? Isabella was loath to figure out if this was the truth. And how many more women would pop up after her?

As a child, she had watched her single mother play this game with the guy who was supposedly Isabella's father. The other women embarrassing her mom at work, on the street, at their apartment. The denials, with her mother letting him come back over and over. All this led to job losses due to loud women showing up at her mother's job, and apartment evictions from physical fights with the lying man. Isabella swore she would *never* play that kind of game with *any* man.

"Thanks for the information," Isabella blurted, trying to get into her car with a little dignity. "I don't have time for this!" Her eyes welled up with tears as she slammed the car door in the young woman's face.

"You just needed to know!" Rena yelled at the closed car door. Isabella picked up her phone and started blocking Jon everywhere...

I am too old for this!

Chapter 3

<hr>

Jamison stepped through the front gate of the house and turned on her watch to measure her exercise stats. It was a brisk day in December, which made her walk more invigorating. Her goal today was 1.5 miles. Jamie turned left outside the property to explore the scenic neighborhood area. She still didn't know all the community residents as she had only lived here during the holidays when she was younger. Some neighbors had come over to the house after the birthday soirée, so she had met some of the newest residents. There weren't any other people walking on the street right now, so Jamie had some solitude.

Her watch beeped with a message from her brother, who asked if she wanted to meet for lunch today. He had something to discuss. It likely involved a girl, but having lunch together would be fun. She paused to reply. As she typed on the tiny watch keyboard, she noticed she was standing in front of the Tolbin home. The older man had lived there for years, and she remembered Mr. and Mrs. Tolbin from her visits to her parents' house in college. Gregory told Jamie that the man's wife had passed away recently and that he was struggling to cope. His children tried to visit as often as they could, but he seemed to be alone a lot. Jamie made a mental note to either invite him over or take him some baked goods from their housekeeper, Olivia.

After finishing her message to Jon, she resumed her walk for another few hundred feet. Then her phone rang (busy morning!)—it was Nick. Her heart fluttered. She had loved the sound of his voice since the night they met. She hadn't felt this goofy in a relationship since she first met her ex-fiancé, Eddie.

Detective Nick Marshall and Jamison Jones Scott met at the initial interview after Rachel's murder. Despite the seriousness of the situation, Jamie's attraction to the six-foot-four detective with the dark, curly hair, broad shoulders, and blue-gray eyes, was immediate. During the case, the pair could not keep their eyes—or other body parts—off each other. Much to the chagrin of her mother. The timing was unfortunate, because solving the murder of their employee was important, but getting to know the detective was too.

"Hello!" she said. They hadn't seen each other in person since the day after her kidnapping. However, they had spoken via video a few times before he left to visit his parents. No phone or video sex happened during those calls, but the physical attraction was a powerful undercurrent of their interactions. *Lots of innuendo...*

"Hi, Jamison," Nick answered in a low voice. "How are you?"

Again, that voice...her nipples tightened, just hearing it. "I'm walking around the neighborhood. Escaping the house and my mother for a few minutes. When did you get back from Florida?"

Typically, Nick would have spent the holidays with his daughter from his first marriage, Gabby. But this year, she was in Europe with his ex-wife and her husband over the holidays. Nick and his siblings made plans for a gathering in Florida with their parents, who had moved there after their retirement. Nick took a quick flight to Florida to visit for a few days. He drove one of his brother's cars back to Atlanta as a favor, just in time for his date with Jamie.

"I just walked into my condo. I left my parents' place yesterday afternoon and drove straight through. However, fortunately for you, I'm still on vacation today and tomorrow, so I can take a nap this afternoon. I think I might need to get my strength up for tonight." He grinned to himself. He had been waiting for this date since they met.

With that statement, Jamie's tummy flipped. Possibly, she needed to rest herself, as she envisioned a long and satisfying night. In an effort to rein in her imagination, she inquired about his trip. "How were your parents? Did any of your siblings visit, too?"

"Mom and Dad are doing well. Not as spry as before, but relatively healthy. And," he added, "Two of my brothers and their families, and one of my sisters and her family, were all there. I'll tell you about the level of commotion with all of us in the house at once. My parents were in heaven, though. Grandchildren galore."

"It sounds like you had a wonderful holiday. How often do you all get together?"

"Not often enough. And one sister was out of the country. But the best part was that she was in Paris at the same time as Gabby and her mother, so my ex was nice enough to take Gabby to have dinner with her aunt. And we looped in my brother, who had to work. We had one big Zoom call with the entire family." Nick smiled at the memory. "My folks were ecstatic."

"I'm glad you spent some time with everyone, especially your daughter." She reflected on her own kid. Jamie rarely talked about her daughter, so it was not common knowledge. And not talking about the pregnancy or the adoption, and the impact they had on her desire for children, had contributed to the crash and burn of her previous engagement. She promised herself she would share this information with future romantic partners but reasoned that it should be an in-person conversation. Especially since Nick already had a child of his own. Hopefully, this discussion would be straight-forward.

Nick continued his train of thought. "I really missed my kid. But Christmas in Europe is an experience I didn't want her to miss. Fun fact: Gabby and her mother are not getting along, which makes sense, as she's now a teenager. I'm waiting for her to try to move in with me because she thinks I'm a softer touch." He paused. "Enough about me. How was your Christmas?"

Jamie laughed. "It was like *Any Given Sunday* at the

house. Along with Jillian and her husband Richard's four boys, Richard's two older sons came for an unexpected visit. The house was wild. The older sons and Jon roughhoused with the four younger kids. Everyone was opening presents, eating a lot of food, making a lot of noise." Jamie laughed briefly and then added with a slight huff, "They all treated me as if I were *fragile*. Hovering around me as if I might *break*."

"Well, I get they were worried." To his credit, Nick avoided adding, *I was too*. He knew from their previous conversations that all the familial concerns stressed Jamie out. He didn't want to add extra pressure. But when he talked to her, when he stood next to her, it felt like he had known her forever. He was falling fast. He would do anything to protect her.

Jamie exhaled. "I know, and it wasn't that bad, really. It seemed weird, though. And it's still going on. Any minute now, my mother is going to call me..."

"Where in the neighborhood are you now? Should I come and whisk you away?"

Jamie stopped and considered the proposition. "Tempting...but Jon called earlier to schedule lunch, and Jillian will call at some point to ask if I want to hang out with the boys." She started walking again, to keep her mind off having Nick sweep her anywhere right now. "I will hold you to the whisking-away portion of the program tonight."

Almost on cue, Jamison received a text message from her mother. *Where are you?*

"Hang on. Let me answer my mother," she told Nick ironically. It had only been twenty minutes since she had left the house, which was irritating—and a mood-killer. There would have been no way to finish her walk in that amount of time—even if she was speed-walking. *Deep breaths*...

She typed, *I'm a couple of houses away. I'll be home in 10 minutes*.

"Sorry about that," she said, as she turned back to her call. "Perfect timing! I have to remember that just two weeks ago, someone nearly killed me. I can't get upset with anyone for caring too much."

"That's good of you," Nick replied with a little sarcasm. "I don't expect the generous attitude to last much longer, though," he said and, after a pause, switched gears back to the purpose of the call. "So, we're still on for tonight? If you are busy or too tired, you can let me know."

Jamie jumped in to answer. "No, I want to go out tonight. I have been thinking about this date, and you, a lot. It's kind of like a new beginning, right? New year, new possibilities?" *Not going to let him back out*...

"I like that. *New possibilities*. I have to tell you, you've been on my mind a lot, too." He paused, weighing whether he should tell her about his talk with his family. *Why the hell not*..."I told my family about meeting you."

Jamie grinned and blushed, but he couldn't see that. "What did they say? Did they approve?" It warmed her heart—and other places—to know that he had mentioned her to his folks.

"What's not to like about you? I'll tell you more details at dinner. Before I get sidetracked again, I reserved a table at a speakeasy-themed bar for tonight. Does that work for you?"

Jamie knew exactly what bar he was talking about, The Blind Pig. Ironically, Jillian had recently mentioned the popular night spot as a location for her next date night with Richard. She would just *love* it if Jamie went there first. "Already have a reservation? Organization and confidence," Jamie chuckled. "That's sexy."

"Is it? It's also blind optimism. Hoping that you wouldn't change your mind." He exhaled. "I'm trying not to sound like a teenager."

"I don't mind. I enjoy knowing that you want to see me. And I have to add that you seem to know people in cool places. How did you pull that reservation off so fast? We only recently decided to go out after your vacation." She started strolling as they talked.

"I know someone who knows someone. Eh, what can I say? How about I pick you up at 6:45?"

"I'll be ready," Jamie answered. "Call me when you get to the front gate." She grew quiet as she started mulling over her clothing options for the evening.

"Hey, where did you go?"

She looked at her watch. *Damn.* "Sorry! I was making plans for what I was going to wear. And no, I won't give you any hints. As much as I would love to continue this conversation, I need to get back to the house. Though, I would rather talk to you," she finished a little wistfully.

"Me too. We can do that tonight. I enjoy talking to you, too," Nick added quietly. "I can't wait for tonight." He took a beat, gathered up some courage, and continued. "Could you wear a dress with a slit in it? I really want to see your gorgeous legs." He ended the call on that note.

Jamie rang off and stared at her phone with a tingly, warm sensation all over. That last statement was cheeky. She liked it. But that sense of calm quickly evaporated when she realized she still hadn't told her parents that she had a date with Nick.

Dropping to sit on his living room couch, Nick couldn't believe he had made that statement about Jamie's legs. Not that it wasn't true, but still. That was bold and new—being this comfortable talking to a woman. He and his ex-wife, Daniella, talked *at* each other a lot, especially near the end of their relationship. That was over a decade ago. Since then, he had gotten comfortable with the status quo. Any relationships that he started ended swiftly, because he had met no one that he wanted to change his life and career for. But this was a different, cool situation.

This was a woman he was willing to work for. He had always said tall women were his kryptonite, and Jamie was five-foot-eleven, so she fit that bill. While she was suspicious and protective when she met him, which was annoying, he couldn't help but notice how pretty she was. And smart...and ungodly sexy...

A brief investigation on his own uncovered some of her past modeling shots and additional information about her background—she was a dermatologist who did medical relief work! He was hooked. When she got kidnapped, he had to balance his concern for her safety with his job...and with one perp, Tatiana, still on the loose, he was still investigating the case. Protecting Jamie from her was a priority.

But tonight was about the two of them getting to know each other. *Hopefully, an evening without chaos*, he mused. *And possibly a little nakedness?*

Just as Jamie approached the house, her phone rang once more. It was Jillian, her younger sister. Four years ago, she had been planning Jamie's wedding and bridal showers when Jamie left town without a word. Jillian took that personally and had taken out some of her long-simmering anger and resentment on Jamie when she came back to town. The sisters eventually came to an understanding, but their relationship had become dicey again after the kidnapping.

"Hi, Jillian," Jamie greeted her.

"You're up early this morning. And you're doing OK? I just talked to Mother. She's worried. Are you going home now?"

It took a moment for Jamison to bite her tongue. OK. *Now* she loathed the gatekeeping from everyone. At least they could be a little more subtle about doubting whether she could walk the neighborhood without someone holding her hand.

"I'm walking back to the house now," Jamie frowned. "Mother knows this. Did she call you to back her up?"

"You know Mother worries," Jillian snapped back "Why do you insist on going out alone? Anything could happen."

Jamie let that wash over her. Anything could happen...in a gated cul-de-sac, in broad daylight? Instead of arguing, she simply asked, "What do you want, Jillian? Are you calling for a reason or are you just being Mother's lackey?" Immediately, she regretted her choice of words. What had started out as a lovely morning had swiftly gone to hell in a handbasket.

Jillian hung up without a word. *Damn, I know she's calling Mother. And now I'm walking into the lion's den,* Jamie thought to herself.

Truer words had never been spoken.

Margaret pounced on Jamie at the entrance to the kitchen. "I cannot comprehend why you are always so cruel and insensitive to your sister. She is only trying to look out for you."

Jamie rolled her eyes, answering as she took off her puffer jacket. "I'm sorry I said that to her. I will call her and apologize. But Mother," Jamie started, "I was in the neighborhood, inside the neighborhood gate for twenty minutes when you texted. I was planning to walk one and a half miles. There's no way I could have finished that in twenty minutes."

Margaret wasn't letting it go. "You almost died two weeks ago. Your decision-making skills are question—"

Jamie interjected. "Don't say it. Everyone makes bad decisions, but you still act like mine are unforgivable! We just talked about this." She hadn't wanted to go there, but again, no one sane thought their truce was long for this world. "You have to give me some grace. I know I was stupid. You don't think I realize that? But I have to have some space."

Margaret shook her head. "Every time I give you space,

you do something foolish. Teenage pregnancy, calling off your wedding, going to a war-torn part of the world, strolling into a kidnapping...you are trying to kill us all. You know your father has high blood pressure."

"Don't do that. Don't blame that on me. Hypertension is common in black men, and his parents both had it. Stop trying to lay a guilt trip on me." Jamie realized she had to rip off the band aid; they were already fighting. Might as well go all in. "I'm going to lunch with Jon today. And Nick is picking me up for dinner tonight."

"That's why you were taking so long on your walk!" Margaret exclaimed. "I knew he was a bad influence!"

Jamie looked at her incredulously. "That's ridiculous! Talking on the phone is a bad influence? You don't even know him well enough to be so judgmental."

"I have my reasons. When you pick a boyfriend, it turns into a mess. You also destroy functional relationships because they are boring."

"You only know of two boyfriends that I have had that ended up in total messes. Just because you didn't know about any other relationships doesn't mean Zach and Eddie were the only two. I don't tell you everything!"

"That's the problem," Margaret said snidely.

"I'm not going to argue with you right now." Jamie turned on her heel and went into the kitchen. In her haste, she ran into Olivia, the family chef and housekeeper. Olivia had worked for the Scotts for years. Both Jillian and Jamie—when she was engaged—attempted, unsuccessfully, to lure her away from their parents.

Olivia handed Jamie a bowl of oatmeal, a plate of

toast, and a green smoothie. She heard the argument and, now acting as an intermediary, turned Jamie around so she could head upstairs to finish her breakfast. Olivia was familiar with the tumultuous mother/daughter routine.

Margaret watched her daughter walk away. She glared at Olivia and stormed back to the master suite.

This wasn't over, she thought.

Chapter 4

Once Jamie reached her room, she mused over the conversation she'd had with her mother. Yes, her relationship with the photographer, Zach, had been a clusterfuck. He was thirty and using cocaine and heroin. She was fifteen, and a virgin, when she met him. Her mother expected her to stay in the model apartment, where she'd have some semblance of support. However, Jamie had moved in with Zach despite keeping her apartment, all while keeping her mother in the dark. On top of that, Jamie was not a natural size zero, so to maintain her weight, she began experimenting with binging and purging, which affected the efficacy of her birth control pills (that Margaret also didn't know about). By the time she turned sixteen, Zach had ODed, and she found herself pregnant.

A mess indeed.

And yes, later in her life she got engaged to a hot,

rich surgeon, but they didn't want the same things in life. Unfortunately, Eddie was not aware of the discrepancies in their respective wishes. She didn't want to have a lot of kids, which her fiancé wanted. He also wanted her to stay home with said kids for a few years. That, too, wasn't something she wanted. She chafed at the restrictions of being in *that* committed relationship. All in all, she wanted out and couldn't find a graceful way to do it—was *there a graceful way?* She left the country two months before the wedding.

While those two relationships had been dumpster fires, she had other romantic relationships in her life. Relationships that were typical and ran their course like most relationships do. Everything wasn't *always* chaos...

After taking a sip of her smoothie, Jamie placed her breakfast on her nightstand. Olivia was a mind reader! Still pissed, she ran some bath water for a quick bath, and called Jon back to complete the lunch details.

"So, what girl is threatening you now?" Jamie led with the most common complaint for her brother. She scooped some oatmeal onto a multigrain toast slice and took a bite.

"Hello, to you, too. Stop chewing in my ear!" he said. "Who have I been seeing?"

"Isabella? Isabella Saldana who works with Dad? Are you messing over work colleagues now too?" She switched to eating the oatmeal; at least, that wouldn't be loud.

"Actually, she broke up with me."

Jamie's mouth dropped open. Not a common situation. Many people considered Jon a great catch, but he had some bad relationship habits. *He* usually ended these short-term relationships. He also fell in love fast and burned out quick most of the time. Mainly because the women were young—*legal,* but young and immature. Jamie thought there was hope that Isabella, who was Jon's age, might change this trend. But it was possible that Isabella saw the writing on the wall and got out early.

"What happened?"

"I'm at the office and don't want to talk about this now. Where do you want to meet for lunch, Jamie Jay?" Jon used the nickname he'd had for her since childhood.

"Something easy. Let's go to Sapori di Napoli Pizzeria," Jamie said, turning off the bathtub faucets.

"Good. I don't want to think about my order! And it's close," Jon replied. "What time do you want me to pick you up?"

"Oh no, no, no, mon frère. I'm driving myself today! My car misses me. I just got it back from the impound. It's back home!"

She could hear an audible groan from Jon. Jamie drove a 1969 Black Camaro. A loud, noisy muscle car that the entire family *hated*. It was a gas guzzler to boot. She had been driving it—at great expense—for around ten years. There had been offers from various family members to purchase her a nice BMW or Mercedes to replace it—but Jamie wouldn't part with the Camaro.

Since her car had been the scene of her kidnapping, the police had meticulously searched the vehicle for any clues about her whereabouts, printing, vacuuming, and evaluating it from top to bottom. Perhaps her family hoped the Camaro would be too closely associated with her trauma, but that wasn't the case. To make it worse, Jamie often leaned into the family's irritation, and kept her early search for an everyday car a secret, planning to only use the Camaro for special occasions. That would ruin her fun...

"Fine, ride in the muscle death trap. Go with God. See you at 11:30," he answered, grumpily, and disconnected the call.

Laughing to herself, Jamie covered her hair and slid into the tub, placing her smoothie on a small bathtub tray that she had pulled out of the linen closet. While in Africa, she had started wearing her hair in a natural hairstyle. Upon her return to the States, she allowed her mother to convince her to flatiron her hair for the party. Two days ago, she had gotten her mother to take her back to Althea, the family beautician, to give her a good wash, conditioning, and a flat twist hairstyle. As she bathed, she decided to leave her hair twisted until the date tonight. One less task before lunch.

So, she had a couple of hours before she needed to leave. Talking to Jon had decreased her ire at the earlier conversations with Jillian and her mother. Nevertheless, Jamie still wasn't quite ready to have a deep discussion with her sister yet. She would deal with the both of them in the new year.

Once again, her life would be filled with new beginnings. When she had returned to the United States, she planned to start a new chapter, but circumstances ended that plan. So, it was time to start again. In many ways, she had a lot to think about.

Best to take this time to hide in her room and figure out what she wanted for her future. She was currently unemployed *and* living at home. Whoever thought she would be in this situation? While she had plenty of money left from her modeling days, she didn't want to spend a sizable chunk of it without a plan to replenish it. If she kept arguing with her mother like this, her folks might throw her out, and she wouldn't have a choice.

Could she move in with Jon?

At 11:05, Jamie crept down the stairs wearing jeans, a t-shirt, and a leather jacket, hoping that her mother had already left for her meeting or remained in her bedroom.

Damn, I should have asked her about the time of the meeting, she thought. As Jamison reached the bottom step, an eagle-eyed and -eared Olivia popped up from the side of the banister.

"You're safe for now, Jamison," Olivia said with a grin. "Your mother left about twenty minutes ago. She was waiting for you, but I guess you know your mother well!" Olivia had heard all the arguing and chuckled to herself again; these arguments between mother and daughter reminded her of when her own children were younger. It made her a little homesick.

"Thanks, Olivia. I'm going to lunch with Jon, so Mother doesn't have to worry right now. I'll see you when I get back!" She gave the older lady a hug and zipped out the door.

The police department had parked her Camaro in one of the garages surrounding the circular driveway in front of the house as a favor to Nick. With the remote, she opened the garage door and admired her car. This car was her first major purchase with her modeling earnings; it would always have an important place in her heart. The black, glossy finish gleamed in the late morning sun. While she had done some initial rebuilding when she purchased the car at an auction years ago, any further, major work could be prohibitive. But the car was so *cool*. And it was a stick shift...

Revving up the engine, she grabbed the gearshift and managed to get to third gear as she rolled out of the circular driveway. Some guys found the fact that she drove a classic manual muscle car extremely sexy. Maybe Nick did, too? She also wondered if her love for driving a stick was tied to its sexual connotations. She *did* like the way the gearshift felt in her hand.

Why am I thinking about this right now? Because she had a date tonight with a guy who made her want to strip down just by looking at her, and because sex might be on the agenda? Because it had been a while? *Maybe that's why...*

They all sounded like reasonable explanations to her.

Chapter 5

<hr>

The lunch traffic that morning wasn't too bad, so Jamie beat Jon to the restaurant. She spent the time sending a text message to her former best friend, and fellow physician, Felice Hoffman.

Jamie and Felice became friends on the first day of medical school and had completed their residencies at the same hospital. Their relationship became strained during the last couple of years of their residency because of Jamie's involvement with Eddie, whom Felice thought was wrong for her. By the time the engagement ended, the two women weren't speaking at all. Jamie wanted to fix this friendship now, too. Since her return, the once-best friends had talked on the phone a couple of times, and had dinner once, before her kidnapping. It was slow going. But as part of the healing process, Jamie texted Felice to invite her to the gathering tomorrow.

Felice hadn't replied yet when Jon appeared.

When Jon entered the parking lot of the restaurant, he honked as he parked next to Jamie's Camaro. Getting out of his gray convertible Mercedes, he strolled around her car, doing a fake inspection. Stopping at the driver's side door, he waited until she opened it, then with a fake look of disapproval, he said, "This damn car..."

Seeing the twinkle in his eye, Jamie started laughing before he could finish; she knew something ridiculous was coming out of his mouth.

"...Looks pretty good for a semi-centenarian. Still very loud."

"You're stupid, baby brother! It's good to see you!" she replied. He wasn't wrong, the car was old...

Jon gave her a hug, then held her at arm's length. "You're losing a little weight. I'm going to make sure you eat today at lunch." He smiled. "When I tell you my story!"

Jamie eyed him. Even if she had to say so herself, her brother Jon-Jon was attractive. Today, he wore a casual suit jacket, a beige pullover, and khaki pants. He was pretty suave, but goofy at the same time. They were only one year apart, and they were closer to each other than either of them were to Jillian. That often caused problems. "Come on. Let's get a seat so you can explain!" she replied.

They walked through the front door of the moderately busy restaurant. After a brief wait, during which they made small talk, a server seated them at a small table and took their order for Arancini and a Margherita Pizza, with drinks. Jamie looked at Jon expectantly.

Jon exhaled and started relaying his tale of woe.

"Isabella broke up with me this morning, and I don't

understand why. We had been going pretty well. I know it had only been two weeks, but we were spending time together, doing adult activities. It was nice."

The waiter brought their drinks.

"The relationship was nice? It's pretty early to go from fire to nice," Jamie replied, sipping on her sweet tea.

"No, there was some fire. Definitely some fire," Jon said thoughtfully. His mind wandered off for a moment—

Likely to a place that Jamie was sure she did not want to visit. *Ugh*! She kicked him under the table. "Hey! You're grossing me out before lunch!"

"Oh sorry! Back to the story. This relationship wasn't like some of my other ones where there was nothing but fire—"

"You mean the ones with the children that you typically insist on dating?"

"Stop," Jon stated firmly. "My heart is broken right now. I'm not used to this feeling." Jon was usually the heartbreaker in these scenarios.

"Sorry. Go on."

"Isabella and I were making plans for New Year's. We just had a lovely night with a carriage ride, and a nightcap at Polaris."

"Sounds wonderful. Did you do something? Did some other girlfriend appear? Did you say something?"

Jon dropped his head. "I honestly don't know. She called me this morning, and everything was fine. Then, within an hour, she blocked me."

Jamie frowned. "Hmmm," she said with sadness. "That doesn't sound good."

"I know." He took a sip of his Coca Cola. "I don't understand. This one was different."

"Oh, Jon, she knows your history. Falling fast, and then sneaking out of the door in the dark of night. She probably was trying to get out before you broke up with her."

"That was the farthest thing from my mind. You were right. I've developed some horrible dating habits."

"Have you been able to talk to her at all?"

"Nope."

"Nothing?"

"Nada." Jon shrugged his shoulders.

The Arancini arrived. Jamie picked one up and took a bite. "Are you sure you didn't *do* anything? Call her by the wrong name? Did she run into Rena or something?" Rena, a student teacher, was the last young woman he dated. Jon had broken up with her right before Jamie returned to Atlanta.

Rena hadn't taken the breakup very well...

The young woman had spent a good bit of time calling their parents' house and Jon's house, too. Rena had also sent Jon a stuffed parrot, intending to make everyone think it was his pet bird. She was acting a little unhinged. Jon didn't help matters by sleeping with Rena again—after the breakup—right before Jamie's kidnapping. The more Jamie thought about it, the more she wouldn't put it past Rena to have spoken to Isabella after waiting outside his house one morning. It had happened to Jon before. Rena wasn't working, since it was the holidays. She could have easily approached Isabella.

"I think it's possible that Rena talked to Isabella today,"

Jamison told her brother.

Jon shook his head. "Do you believe Rena would do that?"

The pizza appeared on the table. Both siblings took a minute to eat a slice in silence while Jon considered what Jamie had mentioned.

Before Jamie could further elaborate on her thoughts, her watch beeped. Text from Margaret. Jamie just passed the message on to her brother. "Jon, please, please, *please* text Mother and tell her I'm with you," she begged him. "Thank you! I'll owe you!"

He dutifully complied as he knew the challenges in the relationships among the women in the family. Jon then took one appetizer and chewed absentmindedly as he sunk deeper into thought. The more he considered Jamie's idea, the more it made sense. He hadn't seen Rena since they slept together. After that night, Jon realized he had made a foolish mistake. He had only gone out with Isabella once before that—at the time, he and Isabella had been nonexclusive. Possibly, Rena had exaggerated that singular sexual encounter to make it sound like it was ongoing.

Jamie finished her Arancini. "You need to reach out to Rena. Did you even have your closure conversation?"

"Not really," he said, as his phone beeped. "Damn Jamie, why are you dragging me into your battle with Mother? Now, she's asking me where we are, and when are you coming home? Oh, here's an oldie but goodie: 'Why is she driving that godforsaken car'?"

Both Jamie and Jon laughed. To see the expression on their mother's face would be worth the price of admission—almost.

"Seriously, Jon. I would try to see if Rena is still in your business. Don't accuse. Be *nice*. Do you even think you can hang out with her for a few minutes without falling into bed?"

Jon rolled his eyes. "I really like Isabella. Of course, I'm over Rena."

Jamie snorted. "That I don't believe. If she flashes some shoulder or leg, you're in trouble. If she flashes her chest, it's over! Your self-control is...hmm." She laughed, then grew serious again. "You need to talk to her in public. Refuse to go to another place. If she admits anything, you can talk to Isabella about it. But you have to be ready for Isabella to be done with you. It's not attractive to have a young girl trailing your man everywhere."

"OK, ma'am," Jon retorted. "Is it better to have a detective trailing you around everywhere?"

"Oh, that's an exaggeration. We haven't seen each other in person since the day after the club of misfit kidnappers snatched me off the street."

"You haven't seen him, sure, but you've talked a few times. Hey, for all I know, you could have been sexting each other while he was out of town. Remember, Jillian and I caught you and Nick almost naked on a bench in the middle of a party?"

Jamie blushed. "Not naked. Not naked," she kept repeating with her hand over her face.

"Fortunately for us. A few minutes later, I would have witnessed something that therapy would never erase." Jon shivered, grabbing more pizza.

No lies told...

Jon continued, in between bites of pizza, "I hate you don't believe me about Rena. I've learned my lesson. From now on, I'll only date women who are mature and aren't over the top."

"Or borderline violent. Psychotic? Irrational? Don't forget the bird in a box situation."

Jon blew right by that. Each word made him feel a little dumber in his partner selection. "I'm tired of hashing through this. Let's talk about you. What about you and the detective?"

"We're going out for dinner tonight. We don't want to brave the crowds tomorrow," Jamie stated, taking another sip of sweet tea. She eyed another piece of pizza. Given her current weight situation, she indulged.

"Does Mother know?"

"Yeah. I kinda told her during an argument, but what's new? She had no time to respond. I think that's for the best, really," Jamie said, sounding braver than she felt. She took another bite of pizza.

"She's had no time to respond *yet*. You obviously got out of the house without her seeing you. But when you get back home, she is going to verbally flay you. I would like to be there for that conversation. I should tell you to go with God because, whew, you're going to need it!" Jon chuckled. He gestured at the pizza, and she nodded as he grabbed another slice.

"I'm still going. I have to maintain my plan of standing up for myself." Jon opened his mouth to disagree, but Jamie held up her hand to stop him. "Please, don't mention the colossal mistake I made with Tatiana, the hapless kidnapper. I may not ever live that one down. But I'm almost thirty-four years old. If I can't manage my life, and survive despite my messes, what's the point?"

"That's true. But word to the wise: you're going to have to move out soon. If you want any chance to live your own life and keep your blood pressure under control," Jon reminded her.

"Mother's coming for you next. If she thinks she has lost control of me, there's you. If Isabella is finished with you, we will be in the same boat. She will try to micromanage your love life. Finish the last slice of the pizza. You're going to need your strength to deal with Mother, Rena, *and* Isabella. Go with God."

"Stop using my line, Jamison," Jon said, exasperated.

Chapter 6

<hr>

Margaret was sitting conspicuously in the living room with a party planning notebook when Jamie arrived home from her lunch. Jamie saw her through the window before she even walked in the front door.

But instead of engaging in or starting an argument, Jamie greeted Margaret quickly, then kept on walking toward the staircase. Determined not to take the bait, Jamie felt proud that they avoided a huge blowout this evening. A sign of maturity, perhaps, on her part. She was glad that Margaret also didn't push the issue either.

Thank God for small favors...

Just because Jamie had gotten into the house without any drama, the young woman knew that she wasn't out of the woods yet. Over the next day or so, Jamie fully expected snide remarks, or some further comments from Margaret, and possibly Jillian, but as long as she had a nice evening tonight, she didn't care. Once in her room,

Jamie started her preparations to take another bath—a long, calming one this time—before her date.

As she filled the tub and added some bath salts with essential oils, Jamie also thought long and hard about her living situation. Jon was correct; she couldn't live here for too much longer. Being an adult, she didn't want to roll into her parents' house late after a date. Or after spending the night out, doing the walk of shame—even if she wasn't ashamed—into the house in the morning. And her living situation led back to her future career. *What was she going to do with herself? Go back to practice, or work with her parents? Be a private investigator? Model again?*

I need to make some decisions early in the New Year, she thought, as she sank down into the tub.

After a brief inspection, Jamie was pleased to see that she didn't need to touch up any private areas—she had dealt with any unwanted hair a week ago through a fairly uncomfortable Brazilian wax. She blushed a little, because she had been presumptuous in even considering such an outcome on a first date. And she probably wouldn't have considered it before the kidnapping, but after all that had happened, there were many emotions swirling around in her head and heart. Life was short.

Jamie also felt a significant connection with Nick. He was sexy and smart. While they argued and bantered, he was protective of her when it counted. They had tried to keep it professional during the case, but the case was over now. Without the constraints of that convention, just a look from those blue-gray eyes could cause Jamie's brain to short-circuit and her inhibitions to disappear.

Jamie also considered that these emotions could just be associated with the circumstances of how they met. Intense relationships often burned very hot and very fast. Wasn't that a line in a movie? Was it *Speed*? Of course, maybe they were both just in it for the sex and would part ways afterwards. Which wouldn't be horrible, *if the sex wasn't.*

As she got out of the tub, she wrapped herself in a fluffy towel and sat on her bed to start the hair untwisting process, which didn't take long; she checked out the preliminary result. It almost looked like a straw set, which was a more tedious process. One day, when she had more time and patience, she would get Althea to do a proper straw set for her.

Next on the list: teeth and face. Preparation status: so far, so good.

Although she had been mentally debating what she was going to wear since this morning, Jamie was still waffling back and forth. She had a choice between showing off her curves—now that she had some—and comfort. Jamie finally decided on a clingy, long-sleeved maxi dress, and heels. During her solitary confinement over the past two weeks, she did a lot of online shopping. Her mother had also bought her several outfits so Jamie could eventually go out and 'find a man'. *Must dress for the role you want!*

Slipping on the dress, she posed in the mirror. The dress was floor length, with a long slit (as Nick requested!), with a gray, black, and white pattern on the mesh material. She had been so excited when she ordered it—a long dress for a tall woman. The fashion world was now making clothes for her height—no more buying XLs strictly for the length.

After making sure her clothes were on point, Jamie carefully applied a subtle face. She didn't use many contouring or other tricks of the makeup trade—only eyebrows, mascara, and eyeliner with a little shadow work. She used minimal foundation (as not to leave a mess on someone's pillowcase) and a pop of red on the lips.

After using a setting spray on her face, Jamie spritzed some Musc Ravageur Eau de Parfum on her pulse points. Musk and vanilla. Hopefully, it was a combination that Nick would find irresistible. She fluffed her hair again and added a platinum chain with a padlock on it, diamond studs, and several platinum bangles on her right wrist. The platinum jewelry was a gift from her ex. *Might as well get some use out of it, right?* she thought, with a twinge of regret.

With her metallic, strappy sandals and her purple puffer jacket, she was ready for her date. Her driver's license, phone, and credit card were placed in an interior pocket of her jacket. *OK, ready to go...*Wait, not quite.

She opened the top drawer of her nightstand. In it was a condom sampler box she had ordered from the website, Lucky Bloke. She needed a doctor's appointment to get back on the pill, but in the meantime, condoms were her most reliable option (as she had a sensitivity to spermicide). An accidental pregnancy was not in her plans; the teenage version of that had been bad enough. She wasn't sure if she even wanted to have kids, so Jamie was going to play it safe.

Hopefully, Nick wouldn't think she was being too forward. After stuffing five (optimistic) condoms into a tiny silver clutch with a chain strap, Jamie did a little twirl in the full-length mirror. *Looks like I could be on the runway...*

Her phone beeped. *I'm here.*

Heading downstairs, she spotted her mother now sitting in the kitchen.

The gamble—should she stop and smooth things over before she went out the door? Or should she just take a chance that her mother would maintain decorum in front of someone outside the family?

Let's go with option 2.

Instead of making a left into the kitchen, Jamie walked towards the front door.

Her decision to go to the door first probably made the decision for Margaret. Jamie knew she would pay for that later. *Oh well,* she thought as the anticipation of seeing Nick again started to build.

Stopping for a moment to compose herself, Jamie paused before opening the door. Surprisingly, Jillian was standing in the doorway, holding a massive fruit basket, unable to open the door herself.

Upon seeing Jamie's disappointed look, Jillian noted, "Nice to see you, too! Excuse me, please." Jamie stepped to the side and Jillian yelled a greeting to their mother. "This is a basket full of treats—fruit, chocolate, and cake. I got so upset today that I decided to treat myself. Then, I thought you probably needed a treat, too." Jillian cut her eyes at her sister, snidely.

"Was that aimed at me?" Jamie snapped back, trying to grab a piece of fruit as Jillian walked by.

Jillian expertly dodged her extended fingers. "None for you! Anyway, I heard you have somewhere to go," Jillian tilted her head towards the door and headed into the kitchen, where her mother was watching the developing scene at the doorway with annoyance and fascination.

Jamie turned, and there stood Nick on the porch. Still as gorgeous as before. Still taking her breath away. He was wearing a black, leather bomber jacket, black slim jeans, black commando-soled boots, and a black, collared shirt. And his curly hair had grown out a little. His blue-gray eyes glinted, and with the jacket hugging his broad shoulders, his jeans gripping his thighs—he looked like a model. Jamie bit her lip...*whew*!

She felt Nick eyeing her appreciatively. *I selected the right outfit,* she thought, gratefully.

All the background noise disappeared when Jamie and Nick locked eyes. They were two ridiculously beautiful, tall people standing in the doorway undressing each other with their eyes. They were oblivious; everyone else was uncomfortable, but unable to look away.

Shit...

"You look amazing, Jamison," Nick smiled at her. Involuntarily, he licked his bottom lip.

Jamie felt herself leaning towards him. *Those eyes were pulling her in.* Fortunately, before she could embarrass herself by throwing herself against him, Margaret harrumphed from the kitchen.

Nick snapped out of his Jamison-induced haze and

remembered his manners, turning his focus to the women in the kitchen. "Uh, good evening, Mrs. Scott, Jillian. I hope you have been doing well," he said.

Jamie moved a little closer to the door and slightly behind him. She was swimming and had to take a deep breath to clear her head.

"Have you discovered any more information about Jamison's kidnapper—that wretched girl, Tatiana?" Margaret asked, squinting her eyes at him.

"We learned some additional details, but we still haven't found her. She seems to be very good at living off the grid. But we will," he reassured the older woman.

"She's still out there. Watch out for my daughter. If anything happens, I will hold you personally responsible."

Nick looked back at Jamie and said, "I would hold myself personally responsible, too."

Blushing, Jamie interjected, "We have to go—we have a reservation." She stepped out of the front door to emphasize her point. "We'll be careful."

"Good night, ma'am. Have a good evening," Nick added, following Jamie's lead. He gently reached for Jamie's hand, which she accepted.

Feeling the heat from their intertwined fingers, Jamie dreamily mumbled goodbye again, and closed the front door behind them.

The scene at the doorway lingered with the two women in the kitchen.

"My, my. That was interesting, wasn't it?" Margaret mumbled under her breath, but loud enough for Jillian to hear. Margaret had long been aware of Jamison's beauty—her daughter had been paid handsomely for it as a teenager. But she was a little thrown at how attractive the detective was. Margaret could feel the *magnetism* between the pair. Which could be a problem. But before she could get too deep into her thoughts, Jillian exhaled loudly in irritation.

She placed the basket on the island, then turned and looked at her mother with a frustrated expression. "Can you not act like everything my sister does is perfection? In front of me, even after I brought you something?" she blurted out.

To maintain her sanity and temper, Jillian started angrily unloading food from the basket. She was already pissed at her big sister because Jamie still hadn't apologized for calling her a lackey. Margaret's actions just grated on her more and dredged up old, lingering insecurities.

Jillian and Jamison's relationship resembled a rollercoaster. The younger sister had felt abandoned as a teen, while Margaret managed Jamison's modeling career. It didn't help that, while Jillian was a gorgeous woman herself, people frequently compared her beauty to that of her older sister's. When Jamie got engaged, it seemed as if there might be hope for a detente between the two. That fell apart. And when Jillian discovered her sister had only communicated with Jon while she was abroad, feelings of abandonment and disrespect sprouted anew. After the kidnapping, Margaret started giving Jamison special treatment again. While Jillian understood why, she felt that resentment about Jamie bubbling up again.

The young woman took a few deep breaths to calm herself down. To smooth things over, Jillian put her hand on her mother's shoulder. "I'm sorry for getting upset. Let's just enjoy some chocolate. It will improve my mood." She held out a piece to Margaret. "Belgian?"

Margaret accepted the candy silently. Watching her youngest daughter move around the kitchen, Margaret wondered how to fix this rift—or if it even could be mended...

Chapter 7

Nick continued to hold Jamie's hand as they strolled to the Tahoe, playing with the pulse point on her wrist with his thumb. He kept surreptitiously looking at Jamie out of the corner of his eye during the walk. The dress showed off everything. Her heels pushed her ass up. *A perfect handful.* And her face—it had been appearing in his dreams over the past few weeks. With the heels, she was almost eye-to-eye with him. *Achingly beautiful.* He could feel specific areas stirring already.

Opening the SUV door for her, he helped Jamie into the passenger's seat; once Nick climbed into the driver's seat, he took her hand again and kissed that pulse point as they drove out of the gated enclave.

"I'm really trying to keep from asking you to skip dinner and come back to my place first," Nick stated, a little hesitantly.

"If you don't try, you never know what might happen..."

Based on how she was feeling right now, Jamie would gladly skip dinner. She envisioned ways of getting out of her clothes smoothly—or she could just keep them on. With the high slit, this dress could be hiked up around her waist and she could wrap her legs around him with her F-me heels still on. She looked over at him and saw that he had the same idea.

But...

While it would be hot as hell to fuck right now, it wasn't the best way to build the foundation of a relationship. Jumping into bed with Zach the photographer had seemed fun at the time, but it had brought Jamie long-lasting consequences. Nothing like a fifteen-year-old learning that her boyfriend shot up regularly, and then being too stupid to leave or protect herself. Everyone in the industry knew about Zach's drug problem, but she hadn't taken the time to find out anything more, except that Zach could give her regular orgasms. She had wanted Eddie, her ex-fiancé, to move faster, too.

Nick had already released her hand and had placed his hand on her thigh. She could feel the heat and electricity through her dress. It wasn't making her thought processes any clearer.

"Wait," she said. Nick looked over at her and removed his hand—much to her chagrin.

"I know this sounds crazy, and Lord knows I want to...but I think we need to go the Blind Pig tonight. First, at least."

Nick remained silent, curious about what she was going to say.

"Oh, I think you're going to think I've lost my mind." Blushing again, she looked in his direction. Not at him, or she wouldn't be able to speak. "I don't want—well yes, I *do* want to, because life is short—but I know I shouldn't just jump into bed...with you." She took a deep breath and dared to look directly into his eyes. *Here goes nothing.* "Although it may look like it, I don't typically dive into bed with my first dates."

Nick snickered, but she could see the pang of disappointment on his face. "Is that what you thought I meant? That's not what we're doing. I intended to show you my baseball collection," he replied lightly.

Jamie gave him a light slap on the shoulder. "Really, I don't. Except for once, which ended really badly." She paused and grew serious. "Listen, I like you. I *really* like you. I've had some terrible experiences with relationships when sex entered the equation too soon. I promised myself that I would try to make better decisions." She shrugged her shoulders. "And two weeks ago, I got myself kidnapped and almost killed. So, I need to work harder on that goal."

Nick ducked his head so she couldn't see his smile. He pulled the SUV into a parking lot of a convenience store to their right. Parking in a spot, but not turning off the engine, he turned to Jamie. "I get that. We can put that on the back burner for a while. I can be a gentleman."

"Don't be too much of a gentleman," Jamie said, in a sexy voice. Then, she added in a serious tone, "Thank you for understanding. And to be clear, I reserve the right to renege on this deal at any time, including tonight. So, just be ready."

"Don't worry. I'm always ready." Nick smiled at her. "We can go at your pace. I want you to be comfortable." He leaned over and pecked a kiss on her cheek.

Why did he have to say that? She almost retracted the deal right then and there...

"Let's get to The Blind Pig," Jamie said, unsure of how the night was going to go or what she was going to do.

The Blind Pig had on-site parking. After opening her door, and helping Jamie out of the Tahoe, they walked arm-in-arm into the establishment. The hostess seated them at a high-top table. With his reservation, Nick got the Holiday package, which included two cocktails, two appetizer bites, and one entrée per person. Their first cocktails came out quickly, while they waited for the appetizers. The background music and chatter made conversation difficult in the festive atmosphere.

"Sorry about the noise. I was told that this was a fantastic place for a first date. I thought that meant you could actually talk," Nick noted, leaning closer to Jamie, so she could hear him.

The warmth of the bourbon in her cider cocktail was going to her head. "It's probably because of the holidays. It's probably a little quieter during the rest of the year." Jamie stroked her ankle against his leg. *Why the hell not?*

Game.

Nick grinned as he took a sip of his drink. *She's*

messing with me, he thought. *Let's see who breaks first.* "So, I have been curious about your time in New York. I saw some of your magazine covers."

"How did you find them?" She repositioned herself in her chair so that her legs were not under the high-top table. Jamie then uncrossed, and recrossed her legs, with the slit of the dress falling open.

Nick tried to ignore the sight of her long, shapely legs. But that was hard to do...

"Mostly through Google. But I do have friends, too. Friends with different databases." Nick smirked at her as she took another swipe at his leg with her foot. "What was that life like?" he continued, trying to ignore her overtures. They had *just* decided to go slow!

"It was a whirlwind, especially for someone my age. By the time I got to New York, my agent was booking me for shows and campaigns left and right. At that time, there weren't a lot of 'influencer' models. You had to see the client and show them what you could do. Had to be skinny—no body positivity, there. Once you had your foot in the door, clients might ask for you directly, and you could skip the go-see part. For some reason, I had the look that the fashion world wanted at the time." Jamie leaned down to adjust the strap of her shoe, giving Nick a direct line of sight down her dress. As she slowly straightened up, she winked at him.

"Th-that sounds like a lot to deal with as a teenager," Nick struggled to focus on the conversation. He stopped talking, as a boisterous and tipsy couple bumped his chair on their way out. They apologized earnestly, without looking at their victim, with eyes only for each other. "Weren't you busy? Didn't you go to school?" he resumed his questions.

Jamie took another sip of her drink, and then pushed her hair behind her ear, exposing her neck. "I had a tutor briefly, but I traveled a lot. I made the lessons up. For almost two years, I made ridiculous amounts of money for a kid. Most of it went into the bank and to investments, since my parents covered my rent. Both college and medical school weren't too expensive, because I got some scholarships."

The appetizer bites appeared all at once and they dug in.

"Do you think you'll go back to work as a doctor, now that you're home again?" They both reached for a powdered donut at the same time, and their knuckles brushed. The second round of cocktails appeared, and the server tried to move their appetizer plates to make room for entrees.

"I really don't know. Maybe I'll become a private eye."

Nick winced. "Oh, then you will be in my business all the time. I might have to arrest you to keep you out of my way."

"Hmm," she licked some powdered sugar from her finger. "Will you cuff me?" *Really?* She got more brazen the more she drank. She knew she was going about this the hard way, but she was enjoying the game.

Surprisingly, Nick blushed at the suggestive comment.

Not going to break, he thought. Unless—maybe he should fight dirty as well.

"You said you were going to tell me about your time in Florida," Jamie stated as she leaned in again to hear him.

He got a delicious whiff of musk and vanilla, which went straight to his head—both of them.

OK, let's play. "My family is very rowdy. We almost sent a couple of members to the hospital on Christmas, during the family football game." While he spoke, he wiped some powdered sugar from the corner of her mouth, giving her face a caress.

Her eyelids fluttered as she realized he was going tit for tat with her. "How did you all manage that?" she asked, taking his hand, and placing one of his fingers in her mouth seductively, swirling her tongue around his finger, and adding a little suction for good measure. "Just getting the powdered sugar off," she said, with a smile.

Set.

Ah, it's on now. "My brothers got a little physical with each other—full body contact. We were playing shirts vs. skins. As restitution for almost decapitating my younger brother, I drove his car back to Atlanta. It's a manual transmission. I take it you can work a stick?"

Low blow. "Of course, I can. I will have to take you for a ride soon."

Sweat popped up on Nick's forehead.

"Oh, *sorry*, I meant in my Camaro. By the way, I wanted to be a cheerleader when I was younger—I was pretty flexible, even though I have long legs. I can still do the splits—both side, and center."

A quick flash of a scene went through Nick's mind: mile-long, brown legs wrapped around his waist—Nick shook his head to clear his mind of the very pleasant image and looked hard at her. "You're not playing fair. I thought we were going to take our time. Is your goal to torture me? It's not necessary. If you want something, all you have to do is ask. If you keep this up, we might not make it back to my condo."

"The two of us? In the Tahoe? I think our combined height makes that almost impossible—SUV or not," she grinned, while trying to imagine the possibilities herself.

"Don't worry. I have an active imagination, determination, and tinted windows. Do you want to try me?" Nick growled, running his hand up her leg through the exposed slit in her dress. Almost all the way up to her thong...

Jamie could feel the heat of his fingers. Her eyes widened as she uttered a soft gasp. *Hell yeah!* The cocktails had fully removed her good intentions. Better decisions could start tomorrow. Jamie stood up next to Nick, pressing herself against him. "Get the check," she whispered into his ear, and blazed a trail of kisses down his neck.

Nick flagged down the next server who walked by—*was this person even their server? Who cares!*—to get the hell out of there. He pulled Jamie closer as the server handed him the receipt for him to sign, which he did...with his non-dominant hand.

Game, set, match.

The two cocktails a piece that they each drank without eating anything substantial, left them both feeling a little buzzed, as they walked out of the establishment, hand in hand. They were giving each other small, flirtatious kisses; each kiss made the trip across the parking lot longer. Did they really need to be driving right now? *All the more reason to fuck in the car.*

As they reached the middle of the parking lot, Jamie stopped walking and pulled Nick toward her. She wrapped her arms around his neck, stretched up, and whispered in his ear, "I can't wait to see your imagination run wild. I have some ideas about the SUV as well."

Nick pressed her close and lowered his head to claim her mouth. However, just as he did, a young man bumped against Jamie, snatched her clutch bag, and darted off. With her arms around Nick's neck, the bag wasn't going anywhere without the chain strap breaking.

And the chain held. Still, the force of the young man jerking on the bag almost dragged both of them to the ground. With much effort, Nick kept the pair upright.

"Hey!" Nick yelled. By the time he and Jamie were steady on their feet, the young man had already let go of the purse and jumped into a waiting car. Nick had gotten a glimpse of the car but hadn't caught the entire plate number.

Jamie's arms had gone from gently wrapped around Nick's neck to her hands in tight fists, clutching at his jacket. He tried to disengage her hands, but she simply grabbed him tighter, saying, "No!"

"Jamie, baby, are you OK? Are you hurt?" Nick asked,

keeping one arm around her. The endearment 'baby' slipped out unexpectedly, surprising him, but he couldn't dwell on the reasons right then, not when he could feel her shaking.

Some club patrons who had been milling around outside gathered around the detective, providing information—which was both good and bad.

"Hold on, please. Can't you see she's shaken up?" he requested. Another person ran over to the group with a chair. "Take it over there, not in the middle of the parking lot. Thanks," Nick instructed the Good Samaritan. He carefully corralled Jamie over to the chair.

At this point, he was able to unwrap her arms from around him. Kissing the side of her head as he lowered her to the seat, Nick realized she was quietly crying.

Shit...

Crouching down beside her, he pulled out his phone to call in the attempted mugging, giving the dispatcher a partial license plate number. Two patrol officers were in the neighborhood; they sped over to gather witness statements and canvass the area. Once Nick had directed the patrol officers, he turned his attention back to Jamie.

Lifting her chin to make eye contact, he asked again, "Are you OK? Let's take you to the ER to get checked out."

Jamie found her voice and replied, "I'm physically fine. I might have a bruise on my arm from the chain." Jamie looked at him sorrowfully. "What the hell is happening to me? Why am I being targeted? Is karma coming to kick my ass?"

"Have you done enough bad shit to have karma come

after you?" He could see her breathing start to regulate, but he kept his arm around her.

Jamie sniffled and snorted at the same time. "It depends on who you ask. There are some people who believe I deserve this bad shit. Just ask my ex-fiancé."

"I doubt it," Nick answered, kissing her cheek, tasting the salty trail of her tears.

She turned her face, so their lips were only inches apart. Even with a tear-streaked face, she was still gorgeous; but her forlorn expression ripped at his heart.

"This is oh-so sexy, huh? Having your date get mugged, and then cry. I wouldn't blame you if you decided I was too much trouble," she noted.

This time, Nick kissed her on the lips. "Watch what you say about my girl," he said. "Can you walk to the car, or should I carry you? I don't want you sitting out here because it's cold. I also need to find out what's going on, so I need you some place safer."

"No, thanks. I can walk. But I will remember that you offered in the future. Guys don't offer to pick up my five-eleven self often," she said with a little chuckle, trying to lighten the mood.

Nick wasn't fooled, because he could still feel her hands trembling as he held them. He helped her stand and walked with her to the Tahoe, supporting her as needed. After helping Jamie into the passenger's seat, he started the car and activated the heat and heated seat. "I'll be right here, if you need anything," he told her, looking into her eyes as he gently cradled her face with his hand. Then he closed the SUV door, while remaining only a couple feet outside of it.

One officer approached Nick. The young man looked familiar but was not a close acquaintance. However, the young officer had recognized Jamie from the case a few weeks ago.

"Your date is turning into a crime magnet," the young man said in a joking manner. But upon seeing Nick's pissed-off face, he ducked his head and shifted his feet uncomfortably.

Nick ignored the man's contrition and looked back at the woman in the car. She had covered her face with both hands. He agreed Jamie certainly had been having a crime-filled December. Nick had to wonder if these events were connected, given that her name had been splashed across the news a couple of weeks ago and the primary culprit of the kidnapping still evaded arrest. *Was Jamie being targeted?*

"You can crack jokes, but you might be right," he replied to the embarrassed officer.

After listening to witness statements for almost an hour, Nick promised to fill out the remaining paperwork in the morning, because he wanted to get Jamie home. They left the bar's parking lot in a much less sexy mood. Jamie had calmed down significantly. In fact, she seemed almost closed off. The pair rode along in silence for a few minutes, with Jamie's hand resting lightly on his thigh, and his hand on top of hers.

"That really killed the mood, huh?" Nick asked. No response.

"Do you want to talk about it?" He tried again.

Jamie sighed. "Kind of. I don't know. I'm trying to make sense of it in my head. But if I start talking, I might fall apart. And I really, *really* don't want you to see that. Not so soon, at least."

"I get it. But this isn't like you're acting unreasonably. You have had two traumatic events happen to you in what, two weeks? I think you're holding together remarkably well."

"I wanted to show you my best before you learned about my worst. It's a little backward. When I'm really upset, feeling out of control, I tend to eat. A lot," she noted quietly and ducked her head, moving her hand from his thigh to cover her face. "And then I throw it back up. I haven't done that since I left four years ago. But I'm trying to manage my emotions right now, and I'm scared, because I really like you, and you're finding out all my bad traits before I've even gotten to confuse you with some cool moves in the bedroom. Isn't that how it's supposed to work?" She offered him a small grin, even while her eyes glistened with tears. "The model woman image dashed."

"Hey, I'm not going anywhere," Nick said, pausing to consider how to phrase his thoughts. "Actually, it's nice to know you aren't perfect—still a mere mortal in that ridiculously beautiful human form. How about this, I tell you some of my dirt to even it out a little?"

She nodded, curious.

"I have done some shitty things in my time. I got

divorced because I didn't care enough about my marriage to work on it with my wife. My career came first, tied with my kid, but Daniella didn't factor in. I figured she'd be there when I got my shield. But she didn't wait." Another pause. "I *was* a dick. But I learned some hard truths about myself. I wasn't ready to put in the work." He said, as he navigated the SUV towards his condo.

"That actually makes me feel a little better. We both have had ugly endings to a significant relationship—endings that we caused."

Nick thought for a moment. "So, basically, we both know what not to do?"

"Yeah," Jamie replied, dropping her head back on the headrest again. She closed her eyes and exhaled forcefully while reaching out to grab his hand again.

"You're feeling out of control, right? If we talk about what just happened, you may gain some of your control back."

Jamie nodded.

Nick continued. "I have a few concerns about the mugging."

Jamie held up her free hand to emphasize her point. "I think I know where you are going with this. Is this related to Tatiana? I just find that hard to believe. She basically apologized for dragging me into her mess. Besides, she probably went to ground and hid. Or off the grid to some island. I can't believe I got to use the phrase 'go to ground' correctly in conversation," she marveled.

"I'm impressed," he said. "As for the other thing, I'm a detective. I have to consider the possibility. She might want something from you."

Jamie knew that was true, but she didn't want to go there—yet. *Why was crime in her face all of a sudden?* "I can't tell my parents about this. They will have me in shackles. Probably have a microchip inserted," she whispered. Jamie turned to him with a fiery look in her eyes. "And I don't want to go home yet. I need something else to think about. This personal crime spree just reminds me that life is fragile, possibly even more than we think. I don't want to miss out on anything. I want to go back to where we were before. Playful, happy, enjoying each other. Not thinking about Tatiana, camper vans, muggers, none of it. Can we do that?"

Nick raised his eyebrow. "I'm a healthy guy who is sitting next to a beautiful woman that he has wanted since he first laid eyes on her. I could get back there in a flash." He glanced at her. "You do know that we are heading towards my condo," he said. "I didn't think you wanted to see your parents so soon. I want to let you make your decisions about what happened after we got there. You can sleep in my bed, and I can sleep on the couch. Honestly, I really want you to be comfortable with whatever decision you make."

"Thank you for that." She leaned back in her seat and let go of his hand. "But I'm glad that the mugger didn't get my clutch." She opened her bag to show him the condoms. "Everything else was in the inside pocket of my jacket. The cards and my license wouldn't fit with all the condoms."

That made him laugh. "You had big plans for tonight." He visually counted out five condoms. "I'm not sure if I should be flattered or frightened."

"Maybe both?" she replied slyly.

He side-eyed her, and she smirked to herself.

They rode the rest of the way in silence.

Chapter 8

———————————

Arriving at Nick's place, Jamie looked around at the underground parking for his condo. "I didn't know you lived in this area. It seems a little trendy for you," she said with a grin.

"A little. But I got a good deal. I've been in my place for over ten years."

Once they pulled into his assigned parking space, Nick stopped the car and turned off the ignition. He turned to Jamie and said, "I just want..."

Jamie held up her hand. "That is very sweet. You want to give me a chance to change my mind, because I was so upset. I shouldn't do anything rash that I'll regret." She laid her head back on the headrest and chuckled. "I *want* to forget. I want to be in your arms, so surrounded by you that you're all I can think of. I can't let this stretch of really, *really* bad luck take control of my life. I have let that happen before, and it screwed up a lot of things for me."

She turned in her seat to face him; her legs exposed by the slit in her dress again. "I have spent two weeks coming to terms with my near-death experience. I have a long way to go, but I can't let it stop me from moving forward with my life—however awkward it is. That's one reason I wanted to go ahead with our date. I met you, and it's been all about you since." Jamie sighed, shaking her head. "I sound like a schoolgirl."

Nick turned in his seat to look at her. "I guess that's perfect, because I'm turning back into an awkward teen. Usually, I'm pretty confident—sometimes bordering on arrogant—which comes with the territory of being a detective. Now I'm unsure and nervous—I spent way too long deciding what to wear tonight." He snickered. "And it's not just about sex, although I won't lie, you are so *fucking* sexy. But I think you're interesting, obviously caring, kind of funny, and you have some of the most gorgeous earlobes—"

He leaned over and pressed a feathery kiss right under her left earlobe. She turned her head to meet him, and they kissed deeply, exploring each other's mouths. Nick found the slit in her dress and slid his hand up her toned leg, to her inner thigh, where he paused, unsure of how far to go.

Jamie noticed the hesitation and reiterated her decision. "Let's go inside," she whispered against his lips.

They both got out of the car unassisted—there was no need for chivalry right now—and met in front of the SUV. She tenderly placed her hands on either side of his face and kissed him softly. Nick wrapped his arms around her waist and pressed her body against him, while nuzzling her neck. She could feel him against her thigh and resisted the urge to climb him like a tree in the underground parking lot.

"If you don't want to give your neighbors a show, we need to get inside," she stated breathlessly.

Grinning, he draped his arm around her shoulder as they made their way to the elevator. Coming from another part of the parking garage, one of Nick's neighbors entered the elevator with them. It was possible the neighbor had seen them making out by Nick's SUV as she seemed flustered when she said hello. Not wanting to further embarrass the older woman, they greeted her with as much cheerfulness as they could muster. Anxious, the lady made small talk, inquiring about their holiday plans.

Jamie stifled a grin—right now she planned to spend as much of it as possible *under* Nick.

Nick politely mentioned watching football during the holiday. As the woman and Nick carried on a light conversation, Jamie could sense the muscles in his leg against her through her mesh dress. His fingers drew weightless circles at the base of her neck, then slid inside her collar to continue the gentle caresses. This distracted Jamie from whatever the pair were talking about. Nick seemed completely composed as he asked the neighbor about her holiday plans.

The neighbor happily informed them that her family would be coming to town and taking her out tomorrow. Nick suggested The Blind Pig; the neighbor thanked him and said they'd consider it. Jamie giggled.

The elevator finally reached Nick's floor. The lady

wished them a happy New Year as the couple exited. Both wished her the same as the door closed.

"Do you know her? You were very pleasant and focused. My mind was elsewhere," Jamie noted as they walked down the corridor.

"I've seen her around. When the neighbors discover that a detective lives in the building, they are more comfortable. I have stories about minor crimes I have had to solve around here." He flashed a heart-breaking smile at her, and her knees buckled.

Jamie blushed as she tried to cover. "Sorry. Now, where is your condo?" Jamie asked. "And I truly appreciate your level of control here. Without the fear of a public indecency charge, things might have ended differently."

"Don't think that I didn't have the same thought in the car. I have ideas about how to best use the space—front and back seat. It wouldn't have been *indecent*," he added with a glint in his eye.

This trip to the door is too long, Jamie thought.

After a few more steps, he stopped in front of the door to his one bedroom, one and a half bath condo.

"This is your place?" she scanned his face, stopping at his eyes. Their faces were very close, since his arm remained around her shoulders.

Those eyes. Jamie panicked briefly—she sensed this might be the start of *something;* something real. It scared her. It had been years since she felt like this—hopefully she wouldn't mess this up.

"We're here. Any second thoughts?" He cocked his head as he looked back at her. That face that he dreamed about had a hint of uncertainty on it. Honestly, he could barely keep his mind clear as he imagined kissing every part of her. But he really wanted her to be sure that she wanted to take this step with him, right now. He crossed his fingers in his mind.

Looking into his eyes, Jamie took the lead. She pushed him against his front door and slid both hands under his leather jacket, giving his butt a two-handed squeeze as she nibbled on his earlobe.

Nick gasped and closed his eyes. *How did she know that was one of my weak spots?* he thought. Her essence surrounded him. The scent of vanilla and musk. *How did she know?* He was having trouble getting his keys out of his pants pocket.

She didn't make it any easier as she pressed herself against him. Jamie gulped as he returned the favor by grabbing her butt with both hands and pulling her firmly against him. He lifted one of her legs and allowed his long fingers to travel up the bottom of her inner thigh...closer and closer...

Nick grinned, "Just so you are clear who you're dealing with...I have a few tricks too." He let go of her ass and leg and whisked his keys out with determination.

The door opened, and they backed up into the condo, face-to-face. She still had her hands on his butt.

He leaned forward and kissed her ear, then mapped a trail of kisses from her ear to her collarbone.

Once inside, the pace sped up—the *urgency* was real. He slid off her jacket and ran his hands all over her body, exploring the areas that he was too circumspect to at the family party a few weeks ago. Neither spoke; they instinctively knew what the other wanted.

Jamie fumbled with his belt buckle as he shrugged his jacket to the floor. She had never dated someone who could actually lift and hold her up against a wall or door during sex. Suddenly, her dream scenario was coming true: dress up around her waist, tiny thong ripped off, long legs with heels still on wrapped around his waist, his pants around his knees, the condom wrapper on the floor...

First times had never worked out this well for either of them in the past!

After the frenzied sex in the foyer, both took a few moments to catch their breath.

Nick surfaced first. "Wo-o-w." He leaned his head against hers. "Are you OK?"

Jamie looked at him dreamily and smiled as she tried to even her breathing, her legs still wrapped around him. "Yeah! I'm *more* than alright. I do need to put my legs down, though."

He adjusted himself so she could stand.

Her dress cascaded back down to the floor. She then slowly unwound her arms from around his neck and stretched gingerly, like a cat. "I must say, getting fucked against the wall is now very high on my menu," she said saucily, before giving him a quick kiss on the mouth. "Where is your bathroom?"

He laughed, pointing to the master bathroom, which

was beyond the bedroom door. Jamie slipped off her heels and scurried towards it.

Nick took that moment to get himself organized again: removing the used condom, pulling his pants up so he could walk, and picking up his jacket from the floor. Stopping to get two bottles of water, by the time he made it into his bedroom, Jamie was lying across his bed on her side—completely naked.

"I thought you might want some water, but I see that can wait," Nick said in a husky voice. His gaze traced her body from head to toe, stopping to appreciate her perfectly shaped breasts, the curve of her hip, and the small heart-shape that remained after what he assumed was a Brazilian wax.

"Definitely," she replied, opening her arms for him to join her.

Nick sloughed off the rest of his clothing and joined her on the bed. This time, he thoroughly explored and savored her. From the arch of her neck to the angle of her collarbone, past her breasts, and down to her navel, he sucked, kissed, and nibbled every inch. Jamie writhed with excitement as he worked his way down her body. He stopped at the 'Revel in the CHAOS' tattoo on her hip and traced the letters with his index finger. "There's a story here," he stated, continuing his exploration.

Jamie grinned. "Once you...get to know me better—um—you'll...understand," she struggled to complete the sentence.

He paused for a second and levered himself up on his elbows to marvel at her. Before he proceeded any further,

Nick said mischievously, "I love seeing you like this..."

She moaned, "Less talking. Please." The 'please' ended in a whimper.

Chuckling, he put his mouth to better use.

Jamie was still vibrating when Nick lay next to her on the bed, his arms wrapped around her. She looked at him bemusedly and reached for his hand to interlace their fingers.

"You *do* have tricks, Detective," she repeated his warning from earlier. She kissed the hand that was connected to hers.

"You sound a little surprised," he scoffed.

She rolled over to face him. "Well, you never know. Some people talk a big game but provide little action."

"So, I'm not all talk, huh?" he asked as he leaned forward and gave her a playful kiss on the lips.

"No, you have a particular talent." She kissed him again and continued. "I want to know what else you've got."

He pulled himself over her while resting on his forearms. "You have no idea..." And they kissed again, this time with even more enthusiasm.

This time was more sensual and exploratory for both. And as predicted, Jamie spent a lot of her time underneath him.

Afterwards, they lay in the bed, silently, their limbs entwined. It was a little awkward, because they had just shared the most intimate experience that two people could share. The silence was comfortable though and lasted for almost ten minutes. The first to break the silence was Jamie. Or at least her stomach did. After only indulging in the appetizer bites at the bar, plus all the excitement from the attempted mugging, and all the sexual exertion, she was starving.

Hearing the insistent growling, Nick smiled at her. "I take it you're hungry?"

Jamie blushed. "Yeah."

"Let me grab my cell." He looked around the bed at the piles of clothes strewn about. His phone wasn't there. "It's in my jacket pocket. I think I left it in the kitchen." He swung his legs over the edge of the bed, stood up, and strolled into the living room, naked.

It was the first time Jamie had seen him fully without his clothes. Long and lean, he was a little more muscular than expected. A smattering of dark brown hair was centered on his chest. A tattoo of a soccer ball sat on the back of his shoulder. Tight, muscular ass. Large hands. Long feet. Had she not been so hungry, she would have followed him to the living room and christened the couch right then and there.

Before she could decide, Nick ambled back into the room, holding his phone. Jamie arched an eyebrow. The frontal view was as nice as the back view. But she was curious about his tattoo.

"Here it is. I planned to hang my jacket up at some point, but I guess I got distracted, eh?" He noticed her intent gaze. "What?"

She smiled to herself and noted, "You should be glad

that I'm so hungry right now." Sitting up in the bed, she continued. "Since I can't do what I want right now, tell me about that tattoo. Soccer?"

He jumped on the bed and turned his back to her so she could get a better view. There was a name in a script font written across the ball. "It's in honor of my daughter, Gabriella. Gabby. She has lived for soccer for as long as I can remember. She always has a temporary tattoo of a soccer ball somewhere on her body. I told her I would get a permanent one after losing a bet with her during the World Cup. A bonding gesture, especially since I haven't been there for her as much as I should have been or wanted to be."

"That's sweet. But I would have expected you to have more tattoos."

"Well, that's weird. You only have one as well."

Jamie dropped her head embarrassed. "OK. I'm so hungry that I'm not making sense anymore."

Nick turned around. "Let's order some food. I can see what I can do to help you forget about being hungry while we wait."

Promises, promises...

After finishing the Chinese food they ordered, Jamie checked the time. It was almost one a.m. While she obviously did not have a curfew, life would be easier if she returned to her parents' home soon. Nick offered to extend the stay overnight, but Jamie knew that would lead to a lot of additional drama at home. While she sat in the car after the attempted mugging, Jamie had fired off a text to both Jillian and her mother stating that they were having a quiet dinner date and that she would be home after midnight.

Setting expectations for her family could avoid some issues.

Once at her parents' house, Nick walked her to the door like a gentleman and waited until she was inside to retreat to his car. She was grateful her hair didn't take much of a hit, which was surprising, given some positions they were in during their sexcapades. And as expected, her mother and father were sitting up in the living room—supposedly reading a book and listening to a podcast. Jillian had gone home hours ago to her family.

When Jamie came in, Gregory stood up and pulled his ear buds out of his ears. The scientist and researcher with a PhD was tall and trim, with a salt and pepper low afro and beard. Other researchers and companies worldwide used his patents for various products and processes. He also had up-and-coming researchers working with him at the lab. With forensic contracts with various companies and the research, Gregory and Margaret's dream business had become an enormous success.

As for parenting, he was the more composed parent of the two. As a result, he didn't seem as worried about Jamie's whereabouts as Margaret, which was part of the reason that he kept Margaret company while she waited for their daughter. Hopefully, his presence would keep the yelling and disagreements to a minimum. He walked over to Jamison as she stopped in the living room and gave her a kiss on the cheek.

"Did you have a nice date with our detective?" he asked.

"Yes, Dad."

"Get some rest. I'm sure you and your mother have a lot to talk about tomorrow."

"Good night, Mother," Jamie stated as she started up the stairs.

Margaret glared at her husband. He really let Jamie get away with too much. Before she could say anything, Gregory cut her off.

"Dear, she is a grown-ass woman. Almost thirty-four. She is allowed to date." Margaret exhaled; Gregory rarely cursed. "And she is with a detective that we *know*. She couldn't be safer. Let's go to bed." He held out his hand.

Margaret pursed her lips but accepted his hand and stood up. Gregory gave her a warm hug. Although Margaret snuggled into her beloved husband's arms, his attempt at distraction was not working. She was sure that Jamie was 'safe' as far as being injured, but given the detective's interest in her, she wasn't sure about how 'safe' she really was. He wasn't a suitable partner for her daughter. But that was something to worry about in the morning.

Chapter 9

———•———

Margaret woke up New Year's Eve with a mission: to come to some agreement with her daughter. Perhaps Gregory was right. Jamison could date. And since Margaret didn't believe that Nicholas was the right guy for her daughter, she felt confident that this would be a short-term dalliance. So, she needed to not inflame the situation and possibly force Jamison to do something rash to spite her. Margaret didn't really have any evidence Jamison did anything just to spite her, but no matter what anyone said, Margaret believed it.

After dealing with Jamison, Margaret could turn her focus to the New Year's Eve dinner. Obviously, Margaret had done some previous planning. Olivia, who had the next two days off, had left plenty of greens, cornbread, black-eyed peas, ham, short ribs, and other New Year's food which just needed reheating. There were also several desserts planned for the feast. The desserts, such as bread pudding, crème brûlée cheesecake, chocolate mousse cake, and a kid-friendly chocolate trifle, were on order, and would arrive before dinner.

Jillian, Richard, and their four sons would be here to eat and watch football. One or both of Richard's sons, Marshall and Martin, from his first marriage, would likely be there—they had spent more time with their father's new family as their smaller brothers had gotten older. Jon would also be present with his girlfriend. Jamison would also be there—perhaps with her new friend. Margaret liked having her family all together as a message of unity for the New Year. Usually, other people would also drop by, like coworkers or neighbors. Since this was the first time in years that Jamie had been home during a New Year's celebration, maybe a friend or two of hers would stop in too.

Gregory rolled over in the bed when Margaret got up.

"Good morning, dear," Gregory stated, looking appreciatively at his wife. He was going into the office today, but not tomorrow. He rarely took full days off, but when he did, the techs would cover the forensics lab, and the researchers could go into the office as needed. Margaret wasn't going in today or tomorrow. New Year's Day would be a nice, relaxing day spent with family.

"Hello! How did you sleep?" she replied, reaching out to caress his face.

"Pretty well. Just a little concerned about leaving you and Jamison alone today." He grinned at his wife. She was often opinionated, but she had a good heart, and was just as beautiful as the day he first saw her on campus all those years ago.

She couldn't help but smile back. It was love at first sight, and she had to fight her parents and grandparents to marry him. He wasn't wealthy and had attended college on a scholarship.

Margaret grew up in Huntsville, Alabama. Her father, Alexander Jameson, had gone to Meharry Medical School in Nashville and had met her mother, Elaine, who was attending Tennessee Agricultural & Industrial State College—now called Tennessee State University. As soon as he graduated, Elaine dropped out of school and followed him to Huntsville. He was a successful doctor who joined a practice with another African American doctor. The couple started quietly buying a few properties and renting them out; all their efforts led to financial success. Alexander and Elaine's success, a rarity for the time, made them extremely protective of their children. When Margaret mentioned that Gregory and she wanted to marry, her parents refused to pay for or support the wedding, as they didn't believe that Gregory could support her or a family. They were snobbish about it. Margaret could not be swayed. Eleanor, Margaret's older sister, even offered Gregory money to leave Margaret alone.

She and Gregory had a small wedding at a friend's home, and she maintained a low-contact relationship with her parents even after her kids were born. Gregory had encouraged her to not use their treatment of him as a reason to remove them from her life. And as Gregory became more successful, the avenues of communication improved slightly, but Margaret didn't speak to any of her four siblings or her parents just to chat.

When she considered it now, Margaret realized she employed some of the same tactics on her kids as her parents had on her. The methods worked on Eleanor, who initially fell for a young man who didn't meet her parents' standards. Their disapproval succeeded in ending that relationship, and Eleanor married an older, wealthy ass of a man, who she divorced almost eighteen years ago. Margaret contemplated the outcomes for her kids; she had definitely put up roadblocks for Jillian and Richard. She didn't have to do that for Jamison and Edward, since Jamison put the kibosh on that coupling herself. But she believed if her kids were serious about a relationship, they would marry who they wanted, just as she did. Jillian had.

Margaret gently placed her hand on her husband's chest, which he grabbed and lifted to his lips. "We will be fine. I will bring you a cup of coffee so you can get ready for work," she replied while disentangling her hand. She leaned over and gave him a quick kiss on the lips.

As she entered the kitchen to start the coffeepot, she noticed Jamison hadn't come down yet. She was hoping to not have to chase her around today. Maybe she would take a cup of coffee up to her so they could talk for a moment. Once in the kitchen, Margaret also set out the tray of bagels, muffins, and croissants that Olivia had assembled and wrapped before she placed it in the refrigerator yesterday. There was always food out, since her children and grandchildren frequently stopped by the house unannounced, especially during the holidays.

After taking her husband a cup of coffee and a muffin, Margaret made another cup and took it upstairs to Jamie. She tapped on the door once, and then knocked more insistently. A grunt greeted her.

"Come in," Jamie mumbled, sounding like she had a mouth full of gravel.

Margaret gingerly entered the dark room, balancing the cup of Kona coffee. Jamie was sleeping completely under the comforter.

"Good morning. How was your night? Sleep well?"

Jamie pulled down one corner of the comforter. She knew what her mother meant by the comment, but let it go. "I did get some sleep. No nightmares either. Why are you up so early? Are you going into the office?"

"No, I am going to put the finishing touches on everything for the New Year's Eve party. No one refreshed the holiday decorations for the party after everything that happened this month. It looks a little sad, don't you think? I can't present our home like that. You know people will drop in." Margaret placed the mug on a coaster and sat on the edge of the bed. "Oh, if you want to invite Detective Marshall over, you can. Maybe we need to spend time with him outside of him being a detective, to get to know him better."

Jamie shot up in the bed immediately. That quick movement reminded her she had used some muscles last night that she hadn't used in a while! She rubbed her ears with her knuckles and pushed back her sleep bonnet.

"I must be going deaf. I thought you just invited Nick over for the holiday gathering."

Margaret pursed her lips. "Yes, I did. You act as if I have no couth. I have been a little hard on him, although he helped us deal with the dreadful murder and the kidnapping. It's not like you are dealing with an undesirable man."

Suspicion coursed through Jamie's veins. Margaret was not this accepting—not like this. She had either devised a plan to run him off or she expected this to be a short-term relationship.

Before Jamie could decide which option it was, there was a buzz at the front door. Jamie looked at her mother. "Don't look at me. Whoever it is, they aren't coming to see me," she noted.

It was Margaret's older sister, Eleanor, whom Gregory had ushered into the house, and whom Margaret hadn't spoken to in years. Margaret asked—not so nicely—what she was doing at her home.

Before Eleanor could answer, Gregory came over, gave Margaret a kiss on the cheek, and whispered in her ear, "I can take my meeting today by video conference, if you need me to."

Margaret, who had stared at her sister like she had never seen her before, snapped back to the present. She looked at Gregory's face, searching for support. "No, you do what you need to do," she replied.

"I will check on you soon." He leaned in a bit more and whispered again in her ear, "Stay calm. I love you." He walked to the door and looked back once he reached it. This situation was a powder keg.

Margaret nodded and turned back to her sister as he left. "You came alone? No husband? Where is Harvey?" She tried, unsuccessfully, to sound excited to see her sister.

"Harvey is in the car. We weren't sure if you would allow us inside," Eleanor tried to lighten the mood, too. "We don't want to be a burden. If we need to pick up more food because I know you weren't expecting us—"

Margaret frowned. "We have plenty of food. I am having some desserts delivered, but we have a full meal—greens, black-eyed peas, everything."

"Really? You didn't really like that stuff when we were younger."

"That was when I was a teenager. Have we not eaten together for that long?" Margaret laughed to herself. That sounded sad to her ears.

Jamie followed her mother downstairs. She recognized her aunt—kind of. She knew that her mother hadn't really dealt with her siblings much since her parents got married. When they were younger, Margaret would take her children to visit their grandfather and grandmother three times a year. The visits usually didn't go well, with snide comments about choices and marrying down.

At first, Jamie didn't understand the tension. She was

only a kid. But as she grew older, she comprehended the situation better. One visit led to a bitter shouting match, started over something four year-old Jillian was wearing, and escalated to the airing out of their disappointment, and a chastisement of Gregory's poor decision-making in his career. Margaret grew weary of this topic of conversation and stopped taking her kids to see their grandparents. Gregory's family was welcoming, so she settled for that connection for her children.

"Yes. It has been a while." There was plenty of meaning hanging in the air, but Eleanor chose not to ruffle any feathers so soon. She shifted her attention to her niece. "Jamison, you're still as beautiful as ever."

"Thank you, Aunt Eleanor." Jamie wasn't sure what to call her. And she could feel the tension radiating from her mother. It might be best to give them some time alone to talk. "Excuse me. I'm going to get something to eat in the kitchen and let you two catch up. Mother, let me know if you need anything."

"That's a good idea," Margaret replied. As her daughter disappeared into the kitchen, Margaret turned and hissed at her sister, "You better not say a word to Jamison about New York and the baby, because she doesn't know what we discussed. Jillian doesn't know about the situation at all either!"

"Why haven't you told them about what happened?"

"It is in the past. Besides, I would never tell Jillian,

because it is not my story to tell. I would never spread personal information. Something you are very comfortable doing."

Eleanor had the good grace to blush.

Margaret continued, "It's Jamison's decision when and if she tells anyone about the baby. And she doesn't know that you know about the pregnancy or anything about your role in the situation."

"That you tried to keep the adoption in the family?"

Margaret held her hand up and hissed again, "Jamison has just been through an ordeal with the kidnapping. She is finally coming to terms with the adoption, and everything associated with it. That I called and suggested that you or your daughter adopt the baby without planning to tell her? She would never forgive me. And that you blabbed to our family and tried to extract money from me?" Margaret paused and held her hands up in exasperation. "What was I thinking?"

Around eighteen years ago, when Margaret first found out about Jamison's pregnancy, it was too late to do anything about it. Margaret entered panic mode, trying to fix things for her teenaged daughter. Jamison was struggling with an eating disorder, trying to hide the pregnancy and work as a model, while grieving the loss of the adult man who had gotten her sixteen-year-old ass pregnant. All Margaret could see was saving her daughter, who was sinking fast. At the time, Eleanor's daughter, Antoniette, who could not have children of her own, was looking for a way to have her own child. Two birds with one stone, right? And this solution kept the child in the family.

Margaret never considered how Jamison would take that. When Eleanor accepted, then asked for money—continued money, child support money—Margaret had to reconsider. This opened the door for way too much drama and future challenges. When she eventually rescinded the offer, Eleanor angrily told everyone that Margaret's perfect model of a daughter was pregnant, and she was trying to sell her baby to keep it a secret. The elder Jameson family members assumed the worst; they assumed there was some type of morality problem with the Scott family. Margaret had married beneath her and all. The Jameson family took the view that the Scott family was uncaring and morally bereft. The worst part was when the family matriarch, Elaine, crying, stated that she did not raise Margaret like this, that marrying Gregory, someone beneath her, had led Margaret down this destructive path, and that their corrupted daughter, Jamison, probably had suggested this solution herself, so she could selfishly continue modeling.

After that, Margaret had no contact with Eleanor for years, and continued the minimal contact with her parents for believing such nonsense about her. Avoiding those toxic people was the only way to keep Jamison from learning about that part of the adoption shenanigans. Jamison finally had a handle on her feelings surrounding the adoption, and if she knew Margaret had basically tried to barter her baby away to a family member...

And the worst part? No one in her nuclear family—including her husband, Gregory—knew that Margaret tried to keep the baby in the family, either.

Margaret took a deep breath and continued. "And now you show up. What do you want? Do you want money now?" She was making assumptions about Eleanor's financial situation based on the past. Trust was difficult to regain.

"I told you why I came." Eleanor paused and reached for her sister's hand. Margaret pulled back. Chagrined, Eleanor didn't comment on that snub, and continued. "We're getting older, and family is important. We need to fix our relationship." Eleanor scoffed at her sister's assumptions. "Like Harvey and I need money!"

Right then, Jamie stuck her head back out of the kitchen. "Would you like some coffee, Aunt Eleanor? I also pulled out some additional pastries if you wanted breakfast." Curiosity drove her to insert herself in the conversation. Of course, she had been trying to eavesdrop without being obvious.

Margaret put her index finger to her lips and shushed her sister before Eleanor responded to her niece.

"Thank you, dear. That's very sweet. Perhaps I'll get some when I come back in with Harvey. He's still waiting in the car." She headed to the front door and paused. "Oh dear. I didn't ask if we could avail ourselves of your hospitality tonight."

Margaret exhaled loudly, but plastered on a fake smile.

"Sure, Eleanor. Jillian and her family will be here, and Jonathan will also be here. They will use their normal bedrooms. So, you can use an empty bedroom down the hall from Jamison's room. When you come back, I will help you get settled. Let me go refresh the coffee."

Eleanor went outside, and Margaret patted her head nervously as she walked back into the kitchen. She didn't trust her sister any further than she could throw her. And she acknowledged this problem started with her going behind Jamison's back, but her sister had the potential to present a danger to her family and Jamison. And after they had just gotten Jamison back into the fold...

Chapter 10

<hr>

Jamie watched her mother as she moved around the kitchen. Something was wrong. Having Eleanor here looked like it was an enormous problem for Margaret.

"Mother, what's wrong?" Jamie had asked her mother this question several times today.

"Nothing. Just—I haven't seen her in years, and she just pops up. I just don't like it."

"Are you sure? There's something going on here that I don't know about. Why are you so angry with her? What happened? Does it involve me?"

Margaret tried to change the subject as she absentmindedly looked in the refrigerator for some eggs. "Is Felice coming to the house at some point during the holidays?" Total change in topic, which Jamie noticed. Margaret didn't mind Felice as a friend for Jamison, but it was rare that she would inquire about her attending an event unless Margaret had an ulterior motive.

"I invited her, but she texted me back this morning. She can't come this year. She flew home to check on her mother, who fell and hurt her hip." Jamie picked up a croissant to go with her coffee. Maybe now was the time to bring up Nick. A distracted Margaret was a more receptive Margaret, and Jamie had to strike while the iron was hot. "I want to follow up on our earlier conversation. I *would* like to invite Nick tonight. Are you sure that's not a problem?" She looked earnestly at her mother. "I really do like him and would like to see if this might be something."

Margaret's situation with her sister rattled her so much that she lost the will to fight about Jamie's relationship. "Despite my reservations, I have already given you permission to invite Nick. With the bombshell visitors that just fell in my lap, I will grant you an evening of grace. I cannot focus on everyone at once."

Jamie surprised her mother by running over and giving her a big hug. This gesture almost brought tears to Margaret's eyes, especially when she thought about Jamison learning about her secrets.

"Now run and call him. I know you are itching to do that. While you're at it, call Jon and inquire about his plus one."

"Will do. When are the cakes and pies being delivered? Actually, when is everyone supposed to be here?"

"Around five. The food will be buffet style, here on the island. Jon will turn on some mood music, and we will turn on some football, and some of those New Year's Eve countdown shows. It should be fun." That's what Margaret had thought prior to the unpleasant surprise, anyway.

If she placed her sister and her husband in the most comfortable room, they might sleep through the festivities. That would be the best—if least likely—scenario.

Jamie kissed her on the cheek again. "Honestly, Mother, it's unlikely you actually believe that." She grabbed her croissant and coffee and headed back upstairs. Margaret started setting up the buffet area for the guests.

The game plan for Jamie had changed. After reaching her room, Jamie called Jon first, because he needed to clarify his plus one situation, and she needed to let him know about the surprise visitors. He might have some insight into what their mother was hiding.

"What's up, Jamie Jay?" Jon answered on the first ring and checked his watch. "Oh, man. It's still early." He was still in bed but sat up to talk. "Are you home? How long have you been home? Did you creep in around sunrise?" Jon teased.

"Ha! Ha!" Jamie replied, rolling her eyes to the room at large. "For your information, I have been home since around one-thirty."

"Really? That's disappointing."

"Don't be disappointed. We visited the Blind Pig, or whatever it's called," Jamie smiled mischievously, leaving out the part about the mugging. "He has a really nice condo, though."

"Jamison, I never!" Jon stated in a phony, indignant voice. "And please don't say anymore. I don't need to know!"

"You only live once, right? Enough about that. Mother wants to know when you are coming over and are you coming alone?" she asked, taking a bite of her croissant.

"Well. I spoke to both Isabella and Rena yesterday. Isabella is coming with me tonight!"

"Hooray! So, she is going to give you a second chance?'

"Yeah. I have just one. I will be on my *best* behavior."

"How did Rena take it?"

Jon scratched his head. "I don't know. She seemed to take it well. It's one reason that I wanted to bring Isabella to the Buckhead house to ring in the New Year and not my house. I canceled all those other plans I made for Isabella because I don't trust Rena to not come by here. She would *never* come to our parents' house. She couldn't get in the gate."

"I hope you're right. Also, I have some big news for you: Mother's sister, Aunt Eleanor, is here."

"In Atlanta?" Jon frowned. "At the house?"

"Yeah, silly. She and her husband drove to Atlanta, and they are spending the night. Mother is freaking out. It is so weird—a weird vibe for Mother."

"Well, seeing a sibling that you haven't seen in years and barely spoke to—" Jon tried to rationalize the situation.

"That might be true." Jamie popped the last bit of croissant in her mouth. "But there's something wrong. You'll see when you get here." She paused. "Besides, she invited Nick to dinner."

Jon perked up. "Sorry? She actually said those words? The world must be coming to an end."

"I told you! So, what time are you coming?"

"Tell her I'll be there by six. I'll call her too. You know she loves hearing from her only baby boy. I might be able to get some clues about what's going on."

Jamie would have retorted in reply, but it probably was true. Jon got away with a lot of stuff because he was the only surviving boy. There had been a first-born boy before Jamie. Trying to get actual details about what happened to the baby was hard. Whether the baby was a stillbirth, or died from SIDS, Margaret wouldn't say. But the tight leash Margaret had on her surviving kids stemmed from that tragedy, too.

"Well, I'll leave that to you. I have to go. I'll see you this evening."

Jamie then dialed Nick's cell phone number, nervous to talk to him, given what had happened last night. He picked up on the first ring and answered, "Marshall."

Oh, my, that voice. Be still my heart...

"Hi, Nick. I didn't mean to bother you at work. I thought you still had another day off." Jamie sat down on the bed.

"I did, but Ron called me about a new report. It's actually about your kidnapping case. So, I came in." Ron Dixon was Nick's detective partner of over a year; they were finally hitting their groove. Both of them worked on Jamie's kidnapping case and on the murder at the lab. Given that the main perp was still on the loose, the detectives wanted to make sure that they followed up on all leads.

"Are you busy this evening, or are you still going to be at work?"

Nick's ears perked up, and he leaned forward in this chair. "What did you have in mind?" Nick asked in a low voice. Nick's mind jumped to intertwined limbs, soft skin, that face under him—*Focus*! He had to pull himself together or he would have to sit at his desk for a while to decompress—literally.

Ron sat across the desk from him, and when he heard Nick's responses, he knew Jamie was on the phone. Ron dropped his head on the desk and chuckled. Three weeks ago, Nick adamantly denied that he was interested in the doctor. He had been lying to himself...no one else bought it.

Jamison liked the way the timbre of Nick's voice changed, and she was also sorry that the evening's activities wouldn't include what his mind obviously jumped to. "My mother has invited you to our New Year's gathering. There will be football galore, music, and lots of food."

Nick grinned through his disappointment. Time for that later. "That's difficult to believe. Does your mother know you're inviting *me*?" he asked mischievously.

Jamie laughed. "Yes, she's aware. It was her idea, I promise."

"Really? Is she coming around? I guess you didn't tell your mom about last night."

Jamie blushed, just remembering those activities. "No! How can I tell her that? You wouldn't be able to grace her doorstep again! I might not be able to come home myself. My mother and I do not have that type of relationship!" Just imagining having that conversation with her mother? Really, it was unfathomable! Jamie knew her mother obviously had sex with her father...*okay*, this thought train was getting uncomfortable. She added, "Besides, she is already bent out of shape about something else. My aunt, who I haven't seen in over eighteen years, showed up on our doorstep this morning."

"Eighteen years? What's the story there?"

"I don't even know what the story is, myself. We didn't see or talk to them much as kids, but it abruptly stopped completely when I was sixteen or seventeen." The timing made Jamie suspicious about the reason, but she had nothing to go on.

"Would your mother actually tell you what's wrong if you ask?" Nick inquired, helpfully.

"Not likely, I tried that," Jamie retorted. Going back to the purpose of her call, she asked, "Can you come to the house between five-thirty and six this evening?"

"I'll be there. I can't wait to see you," Nick replied in a low growl. He could tell Ron was sneakily listening to every word. He turned around in his chair. "I will be respectful, though. No PDA. See you tonight."

Jamison disconnected, laughing to herself. *No PDA? What fun is that?*

Chapter 11

Jillian, Richard, and their four boys—Ricky, Anthony, Jacob, and Aaron—came over to the Buckhead house at five. Richard's two older sons, Martin and Marshall, arrived in a separate vehicle. The young twenty-something men wanted to drive themselves, just in case they had to abandon this party to find something cooler to do. The younger boys hit the front door running, looking for their grandfather. Richard was carrying an apple pie and a pecan pie that Jillian had made for the occasion. He took the desserts into the kitchen while Jillian went to find her mother. Marshall and Martin headed for the family room to watch television.

Margaret was in the master suite bathroom. When Jillian knocked on the door, her mother answered quickly.

"Hi, dear. Come in. Have you talked to Jamison yet?" Margaret was stressed; she had tried to relax during the early afternoon but couldn't turn her mind off.

"Not yet," Jillian said as she walked into the bedroom. "Oh, Richard dropped off the extra desserts in the kitchen." Jillian leaned against the wall and added, "Where is Jamie, anyway?"

"I think she's upstairs. But before you go, I need to tell you something."

"Is it bad? You look worried. Is it about Jamie?"

Margaret waved her off. It was a bad sign that Jillian automatically blamed Jamison if there was something wrong. That needed to be addressed.

"No. Nothing like that." Margaret paused and took a deep breath. "My sister, your Aunt Eleanor, is here."

Jillian frowned. "Aunt Eleanor? Why? I haven't seen her since I was a kid. What brought her to town? Had she called you? Did you know she was coming?" Jillian started to ramble, which put Margaret further on edge.

She held up her hand to put a stop to the rapid-fire questions. "Not at all. I was just as surprised as everyone else." Margaret began pacing around the room, wringing her hands. "I don't trust myself not to say something inappropriate. So, I have to manage how much time I spend with her. I would love to have a non-chaotic gathering if possible!"

Jillian walked over and gave her mother a little hug. "Well, on that note, I will talk to Jamison, so our little spat won't take over the party."

"Be nice. Both of you have quick tempers."

After giving her mother a side-eye, Jillian exited the room and headed for the large staircase. She also heard the doorbell, which her mother rushed around her to open—it was several of their neighbors coming by to enjoy some of the New Year's Eve festivities. Jillian could hear her husband and stepsons in the family room with her father. They were animatedly debating the finer points of a football game. She smiled to herself. While her father and Richard were not that far apart in age, she liked that Richard always tried to maintain the appropriate deference to his father-in-law. She appreciated the effort that her stepsons were making to spend time with their father and younger brothers. Since there was only a small age gap between her and her stepsons, there had been some initial awkwardness, which seemed to be improving. Jillian heard three of her sons running around in the same room, while her nine-year-old discussed the NFL game with the adults. *Life was good*—she needed to try not to be so angry.

At the top of the stairs, Jillian knocked on Jamie's door. After being invited in, she opened the door cautiously. "Jamie?"

Her big sister stuck her head out of the bathroom in a robe with a toothbrush in her mouth. "Hi Jillian," she mumbled through a lot of toothpaste, turning back into the bathroom to get a towel.

Jillian had to laugh. Jamie looked ridiculous with toothpaste dripping down her chin. "Girl, you are silly!" she retorted.

Jamie came back out, wiping her mouth with a washcloth. "Sorry about that. I didn't expect the dripping. And," she paused, then continued, "I shouldn't have taken out my frustration yesterday morning on you. As you know,

Mother has clamped down on me since the kidnapping. I was annoyed with her, and you were there. Easier to get mad at you than her."

Jillian sat on the bed. "I know I shouldn't back Mother up so much. It's just hard. You get a lot of leeway and I struggle with that..."

"I guess I understand that, but I'm not getting any leeway now. Basically, Mother has all but declared me incompetent." Jamie had put on a sparkly ruched top and a pair of flared jeans. She glanced at Jillian, who had on a printed t-shirt and a pair of black jeans. "You look great! Where did you get those jeans?"

Jillian preened a bit. "I'm trying to watch my diet. I have to get in better shape for when I go back to law school. And these jeans are from Old Navy." She stopped for a moment and rolled her eyes at her sister. "I see what you're doing. You aren't slick."

"Is it working? How do I look?" Jamie asked, patting her hair.

"Where are you going tonight? I thought you were staying here?"

"I am. Nick's coming over."

Jillian's mouth dropped open. Jamie gently lifted her jaw back up with an index finger. When she moved her hand, it dropped back down.

"What the hell? Does Mother know?" Jillian asked, stunned.

"She invited him," Jamie stated over her shoulder as she pranced out of the bedroom.

Jillian hurried to catch up as Jamie started down the

stairs. "What's going on with Mother and Aunt Eleanor?" she whispered. "Where are they now?"

"Mother told you about it? And she didn't tell you anything more?" Jamie stopped on the stairs for a second as Jillian reached her. "I honestly have no idea what's happening. Aunt Eleanor just showed up, and Mother freaked out. She put them into the bedroom suite on the other side of my room."

"We're going to have to keep an eye on her. Where's Jon?" Jillian inquired. The sisters continued down the stairs.

"He should be on his way. He's bringing Isabella, or at least he was when we last spoke a couple of hours ago."

At that moment, the front door opened, and Jon and Isabella walked in, his arm draped over her shoulders. He yelled, "Where's everyone? The party has just started!"

Isabella laughed. She had on a long-sleeved, black sweaterdress, and her hair was in a high ponytail. She looked pretty, and happy. Hopefully, any problems between the two would be put on hold for the night.

Jamie and Jillian walked over to the pair to hug them in the foyer. Margaret also rounded out of the kitchen to greet her son and his new girlfriend. Two of Margaret's friends and neighbors, Kumar and Sumitra Singh, were sitting at the bar; they yelled a greeting from the kitchen. Another neighbor, Mr. Tolbin—the one whose house Jamie walked by every day—was sitting at the kitchen table eating a small plate of appetizers. The Singhs had brought him over, as he probably couldn't get there by himself. Another couple of neighbors, the Bentons, stood by the coffeemaker pouring themselves something to drink; they waved their greetings.

Everyone except Margaret was talking at once as the siblings, their mother, and Isabella headed into the family room. Margaret alerted Gregory about the Singhs', the Bentons', and Mr. Tolbin's arrivals. Upon hearing that, Gregory excused himself and followed his wife back to the kitchen to speak with their neighbors. Jillian immediately shifted into hostess mode and took drink requests for the guests remaining in the family room. She then went into the kitchen to fulfill those orders, and to bring back some snacks. Jamie, Jon, and Isabella stayed in the family room with Richard and his sons.

After another ten minutes, the doorbell rang and Jamie jumped up yelling, "I'll get it!"

"It must be Nick," Jon stated sardonically. "The only other thing she would move that fast for is that damn car."

"Jon!" Richard admonished with a smile. "Little ears can hear you!"

Marshall added eagerly, "I can't say I blame her. I would move pretty fast for that car myself!" Martin bobbed his head up and down in agreement. Jon reached over and pretend-punched Marshall, which led to some playful trash-talk.

Jacob and Aaron had both crawled into their father's lap during this exchange. Upon hearing Jon, Jacob started chanting, "Damn car! Damn car!" The sight of the almost-four year-old mimicking him caused Jon to drop his head in mock shame. Richard tried to redirect the little boy, while his two adult sons contributed to the melee by imitating Jon. Ricky and Anthony started laughing and repeating the offending phrase to each other, while Aaron watched the scene in wonder.

Despite the jokes, Jon was correct. It was Nick at the door, holding two bottles of wine. He smiled when Jamie opened the door. "You're a sight for sore eyes!" he said. His gaze roved hungrily over her face and slim form.

Jamie beamed, pleased with his visual approval of her appearance. "Stop that! Come on in!" she whispered, grabbing his hand and leading him into the house. "You didn't have to do that," Jamie added, pointing to the wine bottles.

"I didn't want your mother to think I had no manners."

Which Jamie had to acknowledge was smart.

Margaret stuck her head out of the kitchen again. "Hello, Detective Marshall. I'm glad you could join us today. Come on in and make yourself at home. Do you want anything to drink? Some guests are in the family room right now, and there are some neighbors in the kitchen with me. Head on in there—Jillian will bring in some snacks and beverages in a few minutes."

Walking over to the kitchen doorway, Nick greeted the guests in that room and turned back to the hostess. "Thank you for the invite, Mrs. Scott. Please call me Nick. Everything looks great." He handed Margaret the bottles, for which she thanked him. Accepting a cup and a can of Coca Cola, he followed Jamie into the family room.

There was a loud cacophony of greetings when the pair walked in. Jon and Nick dapped each other up. They seemed to have bonded when Nick helped Jon with a problem involving Rena a few weeks ago. Gregory stood up to shake Nick's hand.

Jamie and Nick sat together on a love seat and settled in to watch the game between the Steelers and the Packers. But to everyone's—including Jamie's—surprise, the other viewers now had a vocal fan of the other team. Nick was a loud fan of the Packers. There was some immediate trash talk, and then a football debate, which led into a larger sports debate. Surprisingly, Isabella also had great insights on what was happening on the screen; because she had no dog in this fight, she aimed to be a peacekeeper.

Jon expressed his surprise to Isabella. "I didn't know you were a football fan," he noted. Another bonus: gorgeous, smart, hot, and a sports fan. *Could it get any better?*

"I grew up in Texas. I was a cheerleader," she said, turning to him as they sat on a small settee. "Couldn't you tell? I'm very bendable." She smiled sweetly.

Jon face-palmed. Add another positive to the column. She leaned her head on his shoulder and got comfortable.

Amid all the din, Jillian brought in two bowls of chips; smaller bowls of sour cream and onion dip and cheese dip; and a charcuterie tray with meats, cheeses, and fruits, taking two trips. Three of her children attacked the chips and dips like little locusts. Her youngest, Aaron, remained on his father's lap, and Richard helped him with a small plate of chips and cheese. Marshall picked up the entire charcuterie board, and pretended to take it to his seat, which incited another roar of complaints and laughter. Jillian gently shooed him and walked back out of the room to check on her mother.

At that moment, there was another knock on the front door. Jillian diverted her path to welcome the new guests. *Rena?!*

Jillian's eyes widened as she attempted to push the uninvited woman out the door. "What the hell are you doing here?" she barked at the uninvited guest.

"I need to talk to Jon," the young woman pleaded. "I promise I won't cause a scene. I want to start the New Year off right. I need to apologize to him for everything."

"This is a family occasion. Why are you here?" Jillian asked again—more impatiently this time. She tried once more to push the woman back onto the porch before others noticed Rena's presence. The family was going to hear the commotion soon.

After a minute or two, Jamie excused herself from the family room when she noticed Jillian hadn't returned. When she arrived at the front door and saw Rena, Jamie narrowed her eyes and exhaled forcibly. *What a mess*, she thought. "Why are *you* here? I know you told Isabella some lies about you and Jon, didn't you?" Jamie inquired angrily as she joined the pair in the doorway.

Jillian looked incredulously at Rena. "Why would you do that?"

"I love him, and he loves me."

Both sisters had lived through this experience with

young women before. Rena was the latest example of Jon's horrible breakup disasters. Earlier during the breakup, Rena damaged some of his clothes and slashed his tires. Just yesterday, she was inserting herself into the middle of Jon's new relationship. Now she was here at his parents' home.

"If you love him so much, why don't you talk to him tomorrow and not in the middle of our family get-together?" Jamie asked.

Rena was agitated, which made it more difficult for the sisters to subdue her. "I need to talk to him now!" Yelling, she slipped by the women and ran into the foyer. "Jon? Jon baby? Where are you?"

Now everyone in the kitchen could hear her.

Margaret entered the foyer to confront the noisy woman. "What is this? What are you doing here, uninvited? Please leave my house! This is entirely inappropriate," the older woman snapped as she walked up to the distraught Rena. The three Scott women tried to get the interloper to turn and walk back out the door.

The noise from the commotion filtered into the family room, and the occupants streamed out to see what was going on.

When Jon saw who it was, he leaped forward asking, "Rena, what the hell?" He panicked, as he had just convinced Isabella to give him another chance. But now his ex-girlfriend had returned and ruined everything again.

Isabella stepped back from Jon's side. She didn't need this kind of drama in her life. This girl was crazy, and that Jon had dated her made Isabella question his suitability for her.

"Wait, Isabella, I'll deal with this," Jon said and turned back to Rena. "I told you it was over."

Nick moved to stand by Jamie, prepared to step in as a law enforcement officer if Rena continued to create a disturbance.

Rena was in tears. "I'm sorry. I shouldn't have spoken to her," she said, pointing at Isabella. "But I didn't want to lose you."

The scene became rather pitiful and painful to watch, so Gregory and Richard ushered the boys and young men back into the family room. Jillian led their upset mother back into her bedroom suite. To be courteous, the neighbors remained hidden in the kitchen to avoid embarrassing their host and hostess. Jamie, Nick, and Isabella remained in the foyer, along with Jon and Rena.

"I don't want to talk about this with you now. I came over here to ring in the New Year with my family. We aren't together anymore. I'm sorry. Can you please go home?"

Rena grabbed his arm. All pride seemed to stream out of her. "I promise. I will be better," she begged, trying to get him to hug her.

Isabella turned on her heel and walked back to the family room.

"Wait!" Jon called after her, then looked at Rena. "Do you think this will make me come back? I don't get it."

"You said you loved me. We were great together."

Nick chimed in. "You're trespassing right now. The owners have asked you to leave the premises. If you don't leave of your own free will, I will have you removed and arrested." He pulled out his cell phone. "Do you want me to do that?"

"You would let him arrest me?" She directed that comment at Jon.

"In a heartbeat. Please go," Jon said, looking back to find Isabella.

All the fight drained out of her at that point. Rena straightened herself up and pushed her shoulders back. "Fine. I can't believe that you would do that. I thought we had something real." She tossed her head and wiped her tears. "I won't bother you anymore." She glanced around at the others. "I'm *sorry* for interrupting your day."

Rena turned and walked out of the door in a huff. Jon had already started the search for his soon-to-be-ex Isabella. Nick and Jamie remained in the foyer to figure out what to do next.

"How did she get on the property?" Jamie asked Nick as Rena closed the door behind her.

Nick shrugged his shoulder as he considered the volatile situation that he had just witnessed. "Do you want me to take this further?" Nick inquired in response. He gently placed a supportive hand on her back.

"I don't think so. Mother couldn't handle the fuss, and Jon has enough trouble on his hands." She looked up at him, eyes bright with her appreciation. "Thank you for asking, though."

There was a rattling noise coming from the front gate.

Jamie and Nick peered out of the window by the front door just in time to see Rena scaling the fence to get out of their yard. "Your security system isn't on, is it?" Nick queried.

Jamie shook her head in wonder.

Puzzled, they watched the scene unfold. "Jon didn't tell me she was that athletic," Jamie frowned.

"I give her a 7.8 on execution," Nick scored Rena's getaway.

"I give her a nine on presentation," Jamie snorted. "Now we just need the cards with the numbers to hold up." Some of the leftover tension in the room dissipated with their laughter.

Nick looked around the room furtively. No one could see them, so he wrapped his arm around her waist and pulled her close to him, so he could steal a kiss.

"Finally, an appropriate greeting! You feel so good!" he growled as he leaned in for one more kiss, which she returned with equal passion.

Jamie moaned as he lifted his head. She realized she did that a lot when it came to Nick. "We can sneak away and make out a little later," she suggested, standing on her tiptoes for a quick peck.

Someone cleared her throat behind them. It was Aunt Eleanor and her husband Harvey, who had just descended the giant staircase. The pair jumped apart.

"Hi, Aunt Eleanor. I didn't know you were up already." Flustered, Jamie greeted her aunt and uncle while wiping her mouth.

Eleanor stared at the couple, waiting for an introduction. Nick looked at Jamie inquiringly, she gave a head nod and quickly introduced everyone.

"It's nice to meet you, Detective. We heard some commotion down here, and we stayed in our room until it was over," Eleanor said as she shook Nick's hand. Harvey tipped his head to both.

Jamie whispered into Nick's ear, "Let me have a moment with my aunt alone."

Nick offered Harvey a drink, and offered to show him where the snacks and food were. Both men walked towards the kitchen with Harvey looking back at his wife. Eleanor waved him on.

The older woman turned back to Jamie and picked up where she left off. "It's a really comfortable room. Your mother always had the decorating touch." She continued talking as she inspected Jamie up and down. "You don't look the worse for wear. I read about everything that happened to you. I want to hear all the gory details. It sounds absolutely dreadful."

Jamie squinted at her aunt and replied, "I don't think that's a great idea. I'm trying to get *past* it. It was pretty awful."

"Well, maybe that's fair. I would love to hear about what's been going on with you since the last time we saw each other. I want to do the same with the other kids. It's been too long. I'm only trying to catch up with my family."

Before Jamie could respond, Margaret returned to the foyer, somewhat calmer. "Eleanor, you're awake! I know you had a long drive here. Did you get some rest?" she asked. "I apologize for the noise."

Eleanor laughed. "I understand, Sissy." Eleanor let the childhood nickname she had for Margaret slip out involuntarily. "Our childhood home was quite noisy most of the time. Weren't we always in trouble? Remember when we went to that party, the next town over? Ooh, Papa was ma-a-a-d!"

Margaret felt a pang of grief at the use of the term of endearment. The memory from long-ago moved her as well. That journey was an adventure! Eleanor wanted to go to a party that the ass she ended up marrying was attending but had been told she couldn't. The older sister used the thirteen-year-old Margaret as an excuse to leave the house. Eventually, groundings ensued, along with drama with another girl who was trying to marry the rich man, too. Life was easier then. Everyone in the Jameson family was on good terms without all the turmoil. Tears pricked the back of Margaret's eyes.

Just then, for a few seconds, the women managed a moment of connection. Margaret had felt like an adult at that party and had been grateful to her sister because she treated her like a young woman. But Margaret quickly came back to the present. No reason to get lost in memories when there were current issues to deal with.

"Jamison, go back to your guest," Margaret suggested gently. "My sister and I have things to discuss. You will have time later to talk to your aunt."

Jamison nodded and retreated to search for Nick.

Margaret regained her serious demeanor. "Let's go into the study, Eleanor," she requested, leading the way. Eleanor followed without comment.

Once inside, Margaret added, "Have a seat. We need to talk."

Chapter 12

E leanor inspected the study before she sat down. Books filled three walls of the study on the first floor, and a spiral staircase on one side of the room led to a second story filled with even more books. The remaining wall consisted of floor-to-ceiling windows. The study's unique design made it a popular place in the house.

"There are a lot of books in here. I guess your husband was as smart as you said he was all those years ago." Eleanor sat down heavily in one of the chairs in front of the big wooden desk. Margaret sat on the other side and swung her chair towards the wall of windows.

"It's been eighteen years since we really talked at all. Tell me the truth. Why now?" Margaret asked again.

"Honestly, I saw an article about Jamison's kidnapping. You hadn't contacted me or anyone in the family about it."

"Why would I? The last time I spoke to you, you put me on blast with the family, and told them all about our personal business. And made me and my daughter look horrible, grasping, and uncaring."

"I apologized for that."

"So, you have *now*. But much of what you said was a lie, too. You made it seem like I was trying to sell the baby to you." Margaret leaned back in her chair. "You told everyone private information, and you lied for your own purposes, and to hurt me. Tell me why I should trust you?"

"Things were difficult for me then. Frank and I were divorcing. I wasn't going to get much in the settlement. My daughter had found out that she couldn't have children, and she expected me to fix it. She heard about Jamie's baby, and she wanted it. I was desperate."

Margaret shook her head. "It does not matter. You ruined my relationship with our parents before they died. They never forgave me for something I did not do. So again, why are you here? I cannot fix their perception of me. They died thinking that my husband had turned me into a different woman than the one they raised, that I was willing to sell my child's baby to save face."

"I am so sorry! I was so lost then." Eleanor looked up with tears in her eyes. "And I don't know why you called me back then, anyway. It wouldn't have been the end of the world if Jamison had kept the baby. And she seems to have dealt with the baby being put up for adoption."

"What?!"

Both women startled, turning around in their chairs.

Jillian had come in to check on her mother and heard the last sentence. "What are you talking about? Jamie had a *baby?* When was this?"

Margaret dropped her head. *Damn, damn, damn! Exactly what she didn't want to happen.*

"Why doesn't she know about the baby?" Eleanor asked, confused by Jillian's confusion.

"Mother, what is going on?" Jillian asked, a little more insistently. She stopped in front of the desk and faced her mother.

Margaret rolled her eyes at her sister. "I told you that earlier. You just don't listen unless it benefits you," she hissed, going around the desk to reach her daughter's side. "Wait, Jillian. Let me explain."

She touched Jillian's shoulder, after which the young woman promptly recoiled. She was furious. Just another example of Jamie getting away with everything, and no one thinking that she was important enough to be told the details. She turned on her heel and stomped back to the family room with Margaret right behind her. Margaret wanted to stop the confrontation directly ahead.

Once she hit the family room door, Jillian yelled at Jamie. "Jamison, I need to talk to you—now!"

Nick and Jamie were cuddled on a recliner couch. He was trying to explain a football play to her amid all the general family din. When Jillian shouted, everyone looked at her, and Jamie was bewildered at being called out.

"What's going on, Jillian? Can it wait?" She sat up on the couch.

"HELL NO! I REFUSE TO BE IGNORED TODAY!" Jillian demanded, even more loudly. The secrets and lies were coming to an end right now.

Frowning with uncertainty, Jamie turned to Nick and

uttered, "I'm sorry. I'll be right back." Nick stayed put, brimming with curiosity, but respected her privacy. Jamie walked out of the room to meet Jillian. Margaret and Eleanor had arrived in the hall at the same time.

Margaret gently touched her younger daughter's arm. "Jillian, let me talk to you. Let's not do this here."

Jillian shook her mother's hand off and laid into Jamie. "I tell you everything. I bare my soul about my emotions, therapy, everything. I talk about how it bothers me that you are so perfect. And you had a baby that no one knew about?"

Jon, Richard, and Gregory came out to see what all the commotion was about.

Jamie felt like someone had gut-punched her. She had planned to tell Jillian when she returned to town a few weeks ago. Then the murder and the kidnapping happened. It wasn't at the front of her mind right now. She couldn't catch her breath—partly from her sister's anger and partly from having the entire story just thrown in her face.

"So, this was a secret between you and Mother, and I guess Aunt Eleanor. How lovely. Did you even tell Dad?" Jillian turned to Jon. "Jon, did you know? You idolize Jamie. Did you know she had a baby, and I guess gave it up for adoption?"

Jon dropped his head. Jamie told him when she first returned to town. It wasn't his place to tell Jillian, but now he looked complicit. Of course, Gregory was aware of the adoption. He put his arm around Jamie, whose world was being blown apart again with an audience.

With the lack of shock or confusion on her father or brother's faces, it slowly dawned on Jillian they knew the secret already. She gasped.

Richard approached Jillian, and she looked at him with tears in her eyes.

"I cannot believe that everyone knows about this. This was a significant event in your life. It explains a lot. But I hate that I'm the last to know things. If nobody knew, it would have been fine. Does no one think I'm a part of this family? Are there more secrets out there that I *don't* need to know?"

Jamie felt a cold sweat sweep over her. She felt bad about her sister, but she didn't really want to discuss this situation with anyone tonight. It was her story, her business, and she was getting a little angry.

And Eleanor knew? Her aunt was leaning against the wall, looking a little smug. Why was she a party to the messiest part of Jamie's life? She side-eyed her aunt. Why did she know all about this? Her mother rarely contacted her family, so why would she have reached out about that situation? It didn't add up at all.

And Nick...

She and Nick had just started to discuss all the nitty-gritty details of their past lives and having this just splashed out there for everyone's consumption was embarrassing. It remained one of the most traumatic events she had ever experienced, and she was still talking to therapists about it.

Jamie could hear Jillian droning on and on, and Richard trying to calm her down. Jamie shook her head exasperatedly and pushed through the crowd in the hallway. She hooked her hands under her mother's and aunt's arms. "Let's have a chat, you two," she told the pair of them determinedly.

Sheepishly, the older women exchanged glances and reluctantly followed Jamie back to the study.

Jillian attempted to follow, but Richard grabbed hold of her hand. "Let them deal with this. You can ask questions later," he stated.

Once the trio arrived in the study, Jamie gestured to two of the seats in the room and analyzed the abashed look on her mother's face and the apprehensive look on her aunt's. Was that why Margaret was so distraught about Eleanor popping in? There seemed to be more to the story, but she wasn't sure that Margaret would let Eleanor tell her the truth.

"I knew there was something going on between the two of you. Aunt, Aunt Eleanor, Eleanor, I don't even know what to call you—you and my mother have barely spoken since before Grandpa's death. But you two had a critical conversation around eighteen years ago—obviously while I was pregnant. Why? That seems like the last thing that you would tell a woman that you supposedly didn't like or trust."

"It wasn't like that," Eleanor started.

"If you aren't going to tell me the truth, I don't want to hear it. I have had a *hellish* December, and I'm not up for anyone *lying* to my face," Jamie stated forcefully, then plopped down on one of the study couches. Before she entered the room, adrenaline was pumping through her veins. Suddenly, she felt drained and apprehensive, expecting to hear something extremely upsetting. But her new attitude since her return was to tell the truth and deal with her emotions—not hide them—even if it hurt.

A few tears rolled down Margaret's cheeks, which she wiped away furiously. Since this child of hers had returned to Atlanta, she had cried a lot. "Jamison, I am really sorry about this. I was only trying to help," she began.

"Mother, how does Eleanor know about my pregnancy?" Jamie pushed a little harder.

Eleanor spoke up. "We discussed the possibility of letting my daughter adopt your baby."

Jamison shook her head, bewildered. "You were going to give my baby away to someone in the family and not tell me?" She started massaging her temples to combat the sudden pain she felt. *Talk about a horror show!* Her daughter growing up in the family, and then finding out about all these shenanigans...*no wonder everyone in this family needed therapy!*

"OK. Why did this *brilliant* idea not happen?" Jamie asked.

Margaret spoke up. "I realized it was a bad idea." She was angry because her sister was trying to gloss over her role in the drama. If they were sharing truths, all truths would be told...

Eleanor opened her mouth to add more, but Margaret interrupted her. "Everything was a mess, Jamison. I am sure you remember that."

Jamie had to acknowledge that fact. She was almost six months pregnant when her mother had discovered her secret, and she really had no plan for dealing with her situation at all. *Just ignore it and it would go away...*

The revelations about Jamie's behavior had shocked and disappointed her mother, but she stayed focused on the task at hand. "You were in so much trouble, I had to help. I was worried about your future. You were only sixteen. Your 'man friend' was dead. You were traumatized—I know you remember finding that unfortunate man's body. You had an eating disorder. Since you were in no condition to make any decisions, I looked for options. And yes, I didn't discuss everything with you. We have talked about this part before."

"Right." Jamie sank into the couch. Reliving that period of her life was threatening to send her spiraling.

"I called Eleanor to lament what was going on with you. A moment of weakness, if you will. She suggested her daughter adopt the baby, and I considered it."

"You more than considered it!" Eleanor said indignantly.

"Sure, until you asked for money and then told everyone that I tried to sell the baby to you."

Eleanor shut up at that point. *Do I need to pack and get to a hotel?* she thought.

"Making our parents think I could sell my own flesh and blood. They already believed that Gregory and I were living hand to mouth. That Gregory led us down this selfish, wanton path. That Jamison wanted to sell the baby so she could go back to modeling. I realized I couldn't trust my sister or my family."

Jamison looked back and forth between the women in

bewilderment. *Finding ways to make a horrible situation worse*...At least she didn't know about all the background maneuvering. She wasn't sure she could have handled it then.

"My life was out of control, Jamison. Please understand." Eleanor again was trying to explain her destructive behavior. Turning to Margaret, she added, "And I wasn't planning to bring this up again. I was a terrible person back then. Money-hungry, soon-to-be divorced, and broke, running the streets. Everything was about me."

Jamison stood up, not wanting to hear any more excuses. She couldn't imagine what this discussion must have looked like eighteen years ago. Of course, she was angry, but then again, was she *really*? Jamie put this difficult set of events in motion herself. She didn't like that her mother had considered trading her kid within the family, but man, the entire pregnancy issue was still tearing their family apart eighteen years later. The child in question was an adult now! The drama had to end *today*. Everybody did what they did—right or wrong. *It is what it is*...Suddenly, she felt lighter about the entire situation than she ever had. Maybe she was finally moving towards acceptance?

"I should be really, *really* angry about this, but I'm not. I honestly think this is a disagreement between you two. You need to figure out what you plan to do about it. I have to deal with Jillian and Nick. But thank you for putting my reproductive history out there on my second date. Appreciate that!" she stated with a wry grin.

A few more tears rolled down Margaret's cheeks. *Damn this girl, here I am with more crying*! Margaret stood up and held out her arms. "I appreciate the grace here, Jamison. I thought you were going to be so furious with me."

Jamie laughed gingerly. "I have to let this go. Or at least try. You were working with the information available at the time to manage the mess that *I* made. I have to learn to accept that." She hugged her mother.

Aunt Eleanor stood up, looking for a hug.

"Not you. I don't know how I feel about your role in this," Jamison noted. Eleanor wasn't quite off the hook yet. There was more to her aunt's side of the story, and she would find out what that was.

As Jamie headed out of the study, Margaret snickered, and her sister shot her an indignant look.

After her daughter left the room, Margaret looked at her sister. "So, you saw an article about the murder and kidnapping and that made you want to come to see us?"

"I guess I hoped you would reach out to me one day." Eleanor paused. "You know Harvey has been a wonderful influence on me. I was really selfish and difficult when I was married to my first husband. Harvey grounds me more; we don't have all the money that I was used to. I will admit, it sometimes is hard. Then I look at you. You went for the man you loved, and you ended up with it all—kids who love you, grandchildren, a husband who loves you, and not to mention money," Eleanor blushed. "Old habits die hard!"

Margaret pursed her lips. Despite twenty years of

minimal communication, she knew money would always be very significant to her sister. But she didn't want to argue about it now. Quietly, she said, "I fought for Gregory because I knew he was my soulmate. The gentlest, kindest, smartest man I knew, and I knew he would be a wonderful father to our kids. I knew he would be able to provide for us. But more importantly, I would have chosen him, even if we ended up with nothing."

"I didn't think about that when I was marrying the ass. He wasn't a good father, husband, or person. All he had was money. I know you told me to wait—that money wouldn't be enough. I didn't care. He was good-looking and rich. Everything I thought I needed." Eleanor clasped her hands together. "How was it that my younger sister was wiser about love than me?"

"Even as a teenager, I could see he wasn't very nice," Margaret noted. "Speaking of, where is your daughter? You haven't mentioned her."

"Off doing some of the same stupid stuff I did. She doesn't talk to me much anymore. Once she found out she couldn't have any kids, she lost it."

"That's what led to the baby drama?"

"Yeah. Along with everything else, my daughter was breaking down over her infertility. We had spoiled her to death. Never said no. So, when she heard no, she cut off contact with me because her father promised to make her baby dreams come true. He, of course, was moving on to his next wife and soon forgot all about her. Just kept sending her money, which she accepted to squander around the world. He got his new wife pregnant—they had a couple of kids and I think he moved on to another wife." Eleanor paused and shrugged. "I was full of bad choices, wasn't I?

"Well, it's never too late to start over. Maybe I will even reach out to our other siblings one day. I'm too old to hold a grudge. But if they give me any lip, I will rain hell upon them."

Eleanor laughed.

"You think I am joking? I can do it. Ask my kids. They may be too afraid to tell you."

Chapter 13

During this time, Richard had ushered Jillian back into the family room. The food had gotten cold, the neighborhood guests had excused themselves, and no one remaining was in the party mood. Marshall and Martin had also made their escape; this was not the best atmosphere to ring in the New Year. The silence throughout that part of the house was thick.

Jamison gingerly stuck her head in the doorway. Hopefully, her sister wouldn't lob an appetizer at her head! "Is it safe for me to return?" she asked.

Jillian was sitting with her arms crossed, wearing a big frown. Her husband's attempt to ease her anger seemed to have gone for naught. Jamie fought the urge to laugh. Her little sister looked like she did when big sister Jamison would muscle a doll away from her when they were children. Wisely, she stifled that laughter.

Time to rip the band-aid off. Happy New Year to Me!

"Jillian, could you come with me for a few minutes? We need to talk," Jamie requested politely.

Jillian looked at Richard, who nodded, then she got up from the couch. Her arms remained crossed as she followed Jamie to the kitchen and plopped herself on a barstool at the island. The resentment was radiating off of her in droves. Jamie tried to keep her irritation under wraps for the sake of family peace. She could see why being the only one who didn't know mattered to her sister, but she didn't understand the level of anger.

"I'm sorry," Jamie started.

Jillian snorted. "You always treat me like I'm not mature enough to understand anything. This was a big deal in your life, and you didn't trust me enough to share it, to talk to me about it. Knowing the complete reason that Mother was always gone would have been helpful for me." She dabbed a tear. "I thought Mother stayed in NYC so much because she loved you more and didn't care what happened to me. Then when you stopped modeling, Mother was so distracted, sad, and *distant*. I just didn't understand what was going on. But I knew it was still about you."

Jamie felt chagrined, because she hadn't considered that. *I guess that could be a good reason to be angry...*"I'm sorry, Jillian, for not telling you about my pregnancy before. It was traumatic for me. It was eighteen years ago, and I'm still seeing a therapist about it. I literally just told Jon for the first time a couple of weeks ago when I returned to Atlanta. So, it's really not like everyone knew something you didn't."

Jillian uncrossed her arms. "Why was it a secret at all? You know all my business—"

"No, I don't. I only know what you tell me. You're more open about your life. I don't run around telling everyone about one of the most horrifying events in my life."

"I don't get it. It's a pregnancy. You and the father put the child up for adoption," Jillian stopped for a moment, then brightened. "Your kid is around eighteen now, right? Maybe he or she will come to find you. Maybe they will want to meet both you and their birth father," she added, assuming the situation could be dealt with so easily.

"I'm not sure how that would go." Jamie replied reluctantly. Then she caught what Jillian said about the baby's father. "Wait, there are several pieces of the tale you're missing," she stated.

To fill in the blanks, Jamie went through the Zach story—how they met, how fast Jamie moved in, how she lied to Margaret for months, how she found out Zach was doing drugs, how she found him dead, and how she ignored she was pregnant for months. Laid out like that, it sounded pretty bad.

With each detail, Jillian became more and more stunned. She also felt guilty for her behavior earlier. "You were dating a thirty-year-old? Then he died and you found his body? Geez!" Guilt-ridden and flushed, Jillian got up and hugged her sister. "Sorry. I guess we both were in difficult positions," she whispered. "And I could have handled this better."

Jamie was a little teary but maintained her composure. "Hey, I have to tell Nick about it now!" she said in a shaky voice. "He heard the basic gist. He's got to be wondering what he's getting into."

Jillian's blush deepened. "I am sorry to have put you in that position! You know I have an issue with my place in the family. I am still in therapy, at least!"

"Important, but not helpful right now," Jamie said sarcastically, then she gave her sister a little grin, which Jillian returned.

Yet another issue in their relationship to work on, but it was a mini-truce for now.

As they walked out of the kitchen, Jillian grabbed her big sister's hand to offer extra support. Eleanor and Margaret came out of the study a few moments later.

"No bloodshed. I'm surprised," Jamie stated, trying to get her nerve up for her conversation with Nick.

Margaret huffed at her daughters. "Of course not. We just had a nice little chat. Did a little catch up."

Eleanor nodded vigorously.

"Stop that, Eleanor. I am still not happy with you. Now I need to talk to my husband for a few moments. He doesn't know about our—yours and mine—adoption discussions yet."

"Oh no," Jillian exclaimed. "I am so sorry for forcing the issue today. I hope Dad won't be too upset." She looked at her mother with a hint of fear.

But Margaret looked calm and gave her youngest a quick hug. "It will be fine. Gregory and I are fine. He may be annoyed with me for a while, though. But it's my fault." She looked sincere.

Eleanor couldn't resist getting a little jab in. "Margaret, you know Gregory is not going to be angry with you. Unless things have changed drastically, I don't remember him getting mad at you for anything, even when he should have. The stories I could tell about the early days."

Margaret gave her sister a mean side-eye. "And this is why I haven't spoken to you for twenty years!" She whirled on her heels to find her husband. Once again, she was questioning her decision to try to reconcile with her sister. There was nothing from her early days as a married woman that would cause problems today. But the fact that her sister tried to give a false impression in front of her daughters made her wonder if Eleanor's presence in her life was a good idea.

Jillian looked back and forth between her mother's back and her aunt. "Mother, would it make you mad if I spent some time with Aunt Eleanor?" she yelled as her mother walked away. "It's so weird to know almost nothing about our aunts and uncles. I want my children to know their family."

Her mother thought it best not to answer.

Eleanor approached Jillian to give her a hug. She was happy to get some familial validation from one of her nieces. Out of the corner of her eye, Eleanor could see Jamie cocking her head; she would have to work on her older niece over time. Obviously, Jamie was not in a forgiving mood.

"I'm sorry that I missed most of your childhoods and

adulthoods. Your mother and I are going to try to get our family back together," Eleanor added, with tears in her eyes.

Jamie watched the scene with some trepidation. "Well, this is *lovely*," she noted with just a touch of sarcasm. "But I have another problem to deal with. Wish me luck with Nick."

Eleanor asked, "Is that the young man you were with? He doesn't know?"

"We have only gone out on *one* date. The loudmouths in this family told him my business before I was ready to."

Jillian's face reddened yet again.

"Like I said, wish me luck." Jamie repeated and headed down the hall.

Chapter 14

Nick sat on the couch, distractedly watching another football game. The room had regained some of its boisterousness after the tense moments earlier; the children were all eating and talking over each other. Richard had managed to keep the plates of all four children filled during this time of upheaval in the household. He was much more hands-on with his second set of children than his older ones.

But Nick's mind was busy. He had overheard some of the discussion between Jamie and her various family members. He didn't think it was appropriate to ask any questions because, really, he and Jamie had only been on one date. She didn't have to tell him everything about her past yet. He had only given the high points of his own past. And really, did it matter? Unless it was a crime within the statute of limitations, he wasn't going anywhere right now, anyway.

Jamie reappeared in the doorway of the family room. Immediate silence. Even the children could tell some strange stuff was happening today.

"Could I speak to you, Nick?"

In his ridiculousness, Jon said, "Uh-oh. To be a fly on that wall." He was pretty happy. Isabella was still here—which he thought was a good sign. *Was it though?*

But for now, Nick gave Jon a dap and joined Jamie at the door.

"Excuse us for a minute," Jamie stated to the room at large. As she and Nick hit the hallway, she suddenly got very nervous. This was one of her first forays into straight-up honesty. This entire situation was out of her wheelhouse.

She stopped in front of a closed door just out of earshot of the rest of the family. "I have something to tell you, Nick. You probably heard some of it since my family has no chill."

"I heard bits and pieces." Nick leaned against the wall. "This seems like a personal issue. You don't really have to bare your soul to me. We are still in the 'getting to know you' phase," Nick stated reassuringly. He studied her face and could see the fear in her eyes. While he wanted to know the details, he found he wanted her around his life more. He was fine with not knowing if it meant that it wouldn't put their new relationship in danger. A chant of "please, not a crime" echoed in his head.

"I know, but I don't think it would be fair to give you half the story." Jamie took a deep breath. "Here it goes—I had a baby when I was sixteen and gave her up for adoption."

Nick didn't flinch. He suspected that the gist of the story was something like that, but he didn't want to assume until she told him.

"No comment?" she asked apprehensively, when he didn't respond right away.

"Hey, I have a daughter. Why would I be upset about that? I would like to know—one day—the entire story. When you are ready, of course. You didn't have to tell me this right now. We have officially had *one* date—a very, *very* nice, amazing, earth-shattering one—but only one. You don't owe me anything."

Jamie's brows shot up. "You aren't asking me how I could have been so stupid? No judgment?" It was almost astonishing, like the continuation of the enormous weight lifting off her shoulders that started in the study with her mother.

Jamie had spent so much of her life post-age sixteen worrying that people would judge her for her poor choices as a teen, even now, as an adult. Her mother did it regularly. She had conditioned herself to expect that type of response. Jamie didn't have a lot of friends, and most of them only saw the image of the perfect model/physician—not the woman who had been through some shit in her time. That façade was limiting, and Jamie had only recently realized how much.

Then she felt sadness. She hadn't told her ex-fiancé,

Eddie, about the situation, because she had expected him to judge her and not want to be with her. Her desperation to have her mother and everyone else approve of her decisions led her to make a really poor calculation. Given Eddie's family and his expectations, he probably would have reacted in ways that she thought he might have. But she didn't give him a chance to prove her wrong.

Water under the bridge... She was over Eddie. But she had torched so many bridges and people because of those choices. There was some guilt mixed in there, too.

Nick astutely read her face and could guess the range of emotions swirling around in her head. He smiled and opened his arms for a hug.

She gulped. That guilt was going to take some time to work through. But she couldn't deny that Nick was ticking all the boxes for now. She went to him, and he enveloped her against him. It was the first time in a long time that she didn't have a niggling worry in the back of her mind about what someone thought of her.

Let's see how long that lasts...

As midnight neared, the remaining people gathered in the family room to watch the ball drop on television. Jamie, Margaret, and Jillian had gathered champagne glasses from the bar and had liberated the champagne bottles from the cabinet.

"Why are only the women doing this?" Jamie asked, with Jillian echoing the sentiment. Margaret tsked lightheartedly as the men all looked away sheepishly. They didn't get up, though!

Each adult received a glass filled with champagne. The one awake child—Ricky—got a cup of apple cider. He felt proud for making it to midnight as a nearly-grown, almost-ten year-old boy.

Right before midnight, each couple paired together to watch the final descent of the ball. Except for Jon and Isabella. She had stationed herself closer to the elder Scotts, avoiding any proximity to Jon. Jon looked over to Jamie, who had noticed the distance. She subtly shook her head to discourage him from approaching Isabella.

"Five, Four, Three, Two, One...Happy New Year!"

The raucous chant became muted as several of the couples personally wished their significant others a Happy New Year and shared either a kiss on the cheek (Margaret and Gregory—no PDA please!), a chaste peck on the lips (Eleanor and Harvey—too old for all this!), or a more demonstrative kiss on the lips (Jillian and Richard, and Jamie and Nick). Jon scooped up his nephew and toasted him, which excited the young man. Isabella quietly raised her glass to the room in general and took a sip in silence.

Nick wrapped Jamie in his arms. "Happy New Year to *us*. I really don't know what that means, but I like the optimistic attitude," he whispered in her ear.

Jamie didn't know either, but the electricity flowing up her back as he gently caressed her spine kept her from thinking too hard about it. The sparks of his touch flowed through the fabric of her shirt, leaving her warm and bubbly. "Happy New Year to you! I can't wait to see what the year brings us," she replied.

"Hopefully, some normalcy. I would love to get to know you without worrying about death and mayhem."

They both grinned, and Nick bent to capture her willing mouth. The kiss deepened without concern about the suddenly interested audience. Both Eleanor and Margaret gave the couple the eye—shades of old-school mamas—but then their attention was diverted by a more exaggerated display of affection.

Despite dealing with marriage, children, and work, Jillian and Richard maintained a strong attraction to each other after over ten years. "We can't let them have all the fun," Jillian told Richard snarkily, and grabbed her husband's hand, pulling him to her for a kiss.

"Who am I to argue?" he replied, kissing his wife hungrily. He was always ready for Jillian—there was no decline in his game as he got older!

"All *right*, young people. Do I need to send Gregory over to separate you? That includes you, Richard!" Margaret said, trying to get everyone's attention.

Gregory looked at her, bewildered. "Do you think I'm trying to separate any of them?" he asked, pointing at the energetic couples. "I'm an old man." Laughing, he put his arm around Margaret's shoulders. She looked up at him with a small smile. When Margaret told him about her dealings with her sister before midnight, he had been upset, but had stated that they needed to talk about it in the morning. It wasn't worth destroying his time with his family right now.

All the non-kissing people joined in the laughter. Which got the attention of the kissing folks, who then surfaced for air.

"Sorry!" Jamie commented first, gently wiping her lip gloss from Nick's mouth.

Young Ricky took that moment to sneak a sip of champagne from his mother's glass, which she had forgotten on the coffee table. Richard scooped him into his arms, and both parents covered their eldest with New Years kisses and tickles. He fought laughing, because he was way too old for this type of treatment, but he couldn't help himself.

Through the merriment of the crowded room, Margaret looked over at Jamie and Nick.

Given the combustible atmosphere earlier in the night, Margaret had to admit that the detective had acquitted himself well during the various squabbles and chaos. Could this relationship work? Had her daughter found the real thing? Margaret was leery, but she was watching.

Chapter 15

After sufficiently ringing in the New Year, Gregory announced that everyone was welcome to stay put overnight, because there was plenty of room at the house. Although this was already expected, he wanted to make it clear. Margaret echoed his comment and encouraged everyone to indulge in more food and drink.

However, Margaret was not allowing her unmarried children to take their dates to their rooms. Not a surprise, but the situation with Jon and Isabella made it more of an issue. Jillian and Richard had already put the three younger boys to bed hours ago. After an epic struggle, Ricky finally lost his battle with sleep after the ball dropped. Jillian and Richard had their own suite to escape to and would carry the sleeping boy upstairs when they went to bed. Eleanor and Harvey had previously made their way to their suite, happy knowing that there may be some repair of the familial relationship in the future.

That left Jamie and Nick, and Jon and Isabella. Jamie and Nick were fine crashing on the recliner couch and settee, where they had watched most of the games and New Years celebrations. The problem was Isabella and Jon.

After the ball dropped, Isabella told Jon that this was their last date. She confirmed that Rena had confronted her and implied that she and Jon were still sleeping together. Isabella had been open to trying again after Jon assured her that Rena wouldn't be a problem. But Rena's appearance at the house gave Isabella second thoughts. She decided to break up with Jon before her heart got too attached, because he had too much baggage. He was a very sweet man, but his personal life was disastrous. Since then, they had been sitting separately for the rest of the party.

They definitely didn't want to share a sleep situation.

Margaret could see what had happened. She felt bad for Jon, but all the women in the family had warned him about his choices in women. She decided that the two couples would stay in the den and brought down plenty of blankets. Isabella chose a solo recliner that was next to the fireplace and not facing the TV. Jon chose a different one across the room.

It was an uneventful night.

The next morning, blurry-eyed guests awoke to the smell of fresh coffee and coffee cake wafting through the air. As soon as the sun appeared, Isabella called an Uber and left for home. Who could blame her?

Jamie woke up around eight, limbs intertwined with Nick's under the comforter that Margaret had kindly placed out for them. They had watched *Trading Places* with Eddie Murphy and Dan Akroyd, which Nick had found on TV after everyone had gone to their respective rooms. Jon and Isabella had retreated to their separate sleep spots, so Nick and Jamie had the TV to themselves. This was their first experience watching a movie together. While Nick was much more familiar with this film because she didn't watch as many movies, Jamie found his whispered asides hilarious. They giggled quietly under the comforter to avoid waking anyone. In between the fits of giggles, the pair exchanged sweet smooches; it was almost like a chaste teen date.

She crept off the recliner, causing Nick to open his eyes sleepily and grab onto her wrist. "Where are you going?" he asked drowsily, with a sweet smile on his face.

Heart melting...Jamie leaned over and kissed that smile. "I'm getting some coffee. Do you want some?"

"Yeah, that would be nice. Black is fine—I need to wake up. I have to go to the station," Nick replied, scooting up in the recliner. She smiled and headed out after making sure that Jon was still asleep.

Nick's phone vibrated in his pocket. Contorting himself a bit to fish it out without getting out of the chair, he managed to answer on the fifth ring. It was his partner, Ron.

"Happy New Year, Marshall! Are you at your condo?"

"Not yet," he said under his breath, getting up quietly to avoid disturbing Jon. "Happy New Year to you! How is your better half?"

"Mad, because she couldn't drink last night!" he snickered. Estelle, Ron's wife, was a patrol officer, and they had just found out they were pregnant a few weeks ago after trying for years. Although it was early, everything appeared to be going well. "How about your significant other?" Ron teased.

Nick entered the hallway outside of the den and narrowed his eyes, as if Ron could see him. "Very funny. You at the office? What's up?"

"I wanted to give you a heads up. We just got a hit on the license plate you reported from the would-be mugger's getaway car—"

"OK. Anything to it?"

"That's the issue. It was at a red-light camera, so we have an image of the driver—" Ron paused again.

"Dude, what *is* up? Can it wait until I get to the precinct?"

"The driver was Tatiana."

Nick froze. *Fuck*.

D.W. Brooks

AUTHOR, PHYSICIAN, KIDNEY TRANSPLANT SURVIVOR

I have always been an enthusiastic reader. Breakfast in my childhood home was a slow process, as I would read any object on the table—newspapers, cereal boxes, milk cartons, anything with inscriptions. Taking away my books was an effective punishment.

As part of this interest, my cousins and I created a neighborhood of preteen and teenage characters who had adventures and solved mysteries. We drew out this neighborhood, identified where everyone lived, and created character profiles for each one. We were well ahead of our time and wrote many unfinished stories, which ended up in the attic as we got older. After this failed experiment, I still nurtured thoughts of writing my own stories one day.

Becoming an author was an early dream pushed aside by practical thoughts and fears. Hence, I decided to take a more surefire route of going to medical school and residency. While I didn't write my own stories, I spent time writing in a medical and educational capacity.

A health crisis awakened the desire to write again. And with the ability to self-publish, I could see a path to getting my words and stories out of my head and into a bound book others could read and hopefully enjoy.

———————●———————

The author lives in Texas with her husband and children. She enjoys trying to stay in shape, sporadically cooking, reading (still), writing, and working on her blog. She is eternally grateful to the woman who donated a kidney to her over 5 years ago and continues to advocate for organ donation as much as she can.

To learn more about D. W. Brooks and future publications and events, visit https://authordwbrooks.com.